YOU KNOW NOTHING

YOU KNOW NOTHING

Yasmina Din Madden

Stories

Curbstone Books / Northwestern University Press
Evanston, Illinois

Curbstone Books
Northwestern University Press
www.nupress.northwestern.edu

Printed in the United States of America

10 9 8 7 6 5 4 3 2 1

ISBN 978-0-8101-4966-3 (paper)
ISBN 978-0-8101-4967-0 (ebook)

Cataloging-in-Publication Data are available from the
Library of Congress.

For my parents,

Sophia Din Madden and John Madden

CONTENTS

SPLINTER

1.

My mother chases me around the dining room table while my sister Lily watches, frozen in the corner of the room like a demented deer. The edge of the table catches my hip, and I swear I feel a crack somewhere inside me. She is a blur in my peripheral vision, her long black hair lashing out behind her like a whip. I only stop when she does, but I'm ready to keep going.

She lunges across the dining room table, but I jump back. I laugh as she pounds the table and spit flies from her mouth as she screams. "You think you know everything? Nothing! You know nothing." My mother's face, which is beautiful—even I can't deny that—glistens with sweat, and her full lips stretch back in a sneer. "You're a lunatic," I say. I smile because I know this is part of what makes her crazy: that I won't raise my voice, that I won't cry in front of her, that I won't eat her Vietnamese food or follow her rules. "This is America," I tell her. "Get a clue already."

She goes into the kitchen, and I wonder if it's over, if I've won, until she comes back gripping her butcher knife, the one she uses to slice meat for the soup that makes me choke. My hip aches, and I feel sweat collecting at the base of my spine. Even for her, this seems like too much. Outside, I hear children scream *ghost in the graveyard!* Their laughter is far away, but it washes through the screened windows, muted as if we are all underwater. When I was a kid, my mother cried for me when I got hurt. No one has ever cried for me but her.

2.

Stupid girl. And me running after her crazy like a chicken with its head off. Skirt so short and top she cuts to hang off her, make her look like she live on the street. No shame!

Always Elyse thinks she know. Her hair with some little blond from her father. And she puts lemon to make even lighter! No Asian in her. Not like her sisters and brother. They have Asian. They know how to act. "Turn off the soup," I yell at Lily, who watches.

Elyse just keep running. Always going that one. Never home. Never helps. Only with friends all the time. When she's home, only open her mouth to complain! "I won't eat that," she always say. Only cereal she eats. And then she in the bathroom. I know what she doing.

I lean on the table, and she laughs in my face! My wrist aches when I pound the table. "You think you know everything? Chúa ơi tôi sẽ gieết bạn!" She's so stubborn. When she was a baby, she barely cry. Not like my others, who cry all the time, who let me hold them. No. Elyse only cry if it really hurts, so I knew it was bad if she cry. I was always afraid when she little. I was so young with Elyse, and back then I cry with her.

In the kitchen, the soup boil over, broth everywhere, under the burners, dripping on my clean floor. All day I cook and clean and still there's more to do. Help kids with math. Max needs to do his reading. Still need to chop vegetables for dinner! The knife handle is so smooth, and it feels so light in my hand.

3.

Watching my mother chase my sister around the dining room table is like watching a sporting event—not like tennis with its neat volleys and its predictable accumulation of points but more like horse racing: a burst of energy by beautiful, muscled beasts who might, in a flash, collapse in a heap of busted bone and ligament. My mother yells for me to turn off the soup, but I won't move.

They are long and lean, my mother and sister, with straight dark hair that flares out behind them as they lap the table. Who knows what they fight about this time: My sister's smart mouth? Her habit of puking after meals? Elyse calls the Vietnamese food my mother cooks disgusting, which sometimes it is, but it's often good too. That's the thing about Elyse: something can never be more than one thing for her. For either of them. They're exactly the same, really, my mother and my sister.

My mother can't catch Elyse, so she yells in Vietnamese that she's going to kill her. This is the only Vietnamese I know. "You're a lunatic," Elyse tells her. She is calm and smiling in her peach miniskirt and off-the-shoulder sweatshirt. My sister talks to me like this too, and it makes me want to punch her in the face.

My mother goes into the kitchen and returns, gripping a knife—the one she uses to chop bitter melon for the soup I love. Elyse is afraid, though she tries to look like she isn't. My older sister is hard. But it's true that my mother seems crazy. They stare at each other for a moment, both breathing fast. There's a chance my mother won't throw the knife, but there's just as good a chance she will. We wait. When my mother flings the knife across the table at my sister, the tip of the blade nicks the wooden surface before clattering to the floor beside Elyse, who has flattened herself against the wall. No one moves until finally I walk closer to the table and see the split in the shiny brown surface, glimpse the raw, splintered wood inside.

A WOMAN OF APPETITES

She was always hungry, so when Adeline ate her beautiful baby boy, no one was surprised. Not her husband or the friends who commented relentlessly on her appetite. "Look how she eats!" "Where does it go?" They exclaimed with delight and horror. "Her legs, they must be hollow!"

"You're insatiable!" her husband often claimed, sprawled naked across wrinkled sheets. "You just can't get enough, can you?" He smiled proudly with such statements. And it was true: she couldn't get enough of anything. She was hungry. It couldn't be helped.

When the baby came, Adeline knew she was in trouble. The tiny boy was utterly delectable. His fat, juicy cheeks, the velvety soft soles of his feet, the whispery tickle of his eyelashes against her breasts when he nursed. She kissed his small belly, his dimpled knees and elbows, his fuzzy scalp, his peachy bum, his tiny, curled toes. She would have kissed his eyeballs if it were easier.

The husband enjoyed these displays of motherly love, especially since they did nothing to dampen her appetite for him. If anything, his wife's appetites had grown since giving birth. In the middle of the night, just hours after they'd fucked, she'd climb on top of him and demand more, and yet more upon waking. He joked he'd have to outsource to meet her demands. When Adeline laughed and said she'd supplement as needed, the husband became just the slightest bit anxious. When he came home to find her astride their neighbor Sid, he was more relieved than angry, though. It's true what they say, he thought as he watched her bucking against his friend, it takes a village.

Between kissing her baby and fucking her husband and the occasional neighbor, Adeline ate, and Adeline read: heaping spoonfuls of peanut butter straight from the jar as she devoured a fat tome on geography and the rise of first world countries; towering sandwiches that toppled over when she set them down to turn the pages of *Anna Karenina*; steak that she ate without cutting, straight from the pan, just a rare hunk speared by her fork, the easier to eat while reading *Mythology: Timeless Tales of Gods and Heroes.*

So, it really came as no surprise to anyone that Adeline woke up one morning and ate her baby. She'd begun as she always began every morning, swinging her little munchkin up from his crib to the changing table and cooing to him as she changed his diaper. Then Adeline kissed him from the soles of his feet to his wispy crown of hair, not realizing until he was gone that she'd actually gobbled him whole. "You weren't supposed to do that!" cried her husband, though he'd known it was bound to happen.

"But of course I know that!" she shouted. "I was just so hungry. It couldn't be helped." And with that, she turned on her heel, grabbed a jar of peanut butter from the pantry, and settled onto the couch with a tattered copy of *Bad Behavior.* "How could you?" he continued to cry. The woman paused and shook her peanut butter–covered finger at him. "Let it go, or I'll eat you too." When the husband brought up the baby again, Adeline swallowed him up in one gulp. Silence at last, she thought, and she drove to the library to check out more books.

When the neighbors realized what had happened, that she'd eaten not just her baby but her husband as well, they whispered "How could she?" and "What kind of woman does that to her family?" "I know she has a big appetite," they exclaimed, "but how much does she need?" Since Sid, Betsy, Michael, Anastasia, Eduardo, and several others were benefiting from Adeline's sexual appetite, these whispers never grew to the roar they might have. Plus, they knew what had happened to Jackson and Sally, Adeline's nosy neighbors who liked to peek at her over the backyard fence and who hadn't refrained from openly judging her. Adeline ate them, one right after the other, with barely a pause after swallowing Jackson, who many considered to be morbidly obese.

In addition to devouring food, books, and the occasional neighbor or two, Adeline had taken to riding her bike for hours at a time. She liked to load up a backpack with cheese, baguettes, jars of cornichons and olives, and cycle out far enough to where the roads turned to gravel, and she could count fence posts and hear the birds. When she got tired, she'd stop on the side of the road and eat everything in her pack. Sometimes she'd read a book.

More often than not, she'd move off the road into the field next to it and fall asleep. And this is how Adeline came to wake up one day to a man hovering above her with a wolfish smile that opened to say "You know you could run into trouble out here alone, lady."

"And?" Adeline replied. His jeans were horribly tight and with his legs spread above her, she marveled that the denim didn't split at the seam. "And?" he repeated. She noticed an unsightly vein pulsing in his forehead. "Well, who knows what could happen. Someone could hurt you."

"Hurt me how?" Adeline sat up and gently pushed on the man's legs, so he'd back up and give her some room. When he grabbed her wrist tightly, she opened her mouth so wide that her jaw popped loudly, momentarily surprising the man before she polished him off. She lay back on the grass, caressing her full belly. Her neighbors thought her a gluttonous monster, an insatiable demon-lover. She laughed to herself. At them. Who were they to judge her? Who's to say her appetites weren't bountiful rather than gluttonous?

AND THIS IS HOW IT ENDED

THE END

Me at his door, trying to convince him I was a good person. But I wasn't a good person back then, needy and egotistical, kind and then poisonous. On his doorstep that day, David told me I was like a creeping bellflower, a weed people mistake for a flower and let run rampant in their gardens. The problem is, he told me, a weed is a weed. I looked up creeping bellflower, and it does have beautiful blue bells crawling up its stalks. It also has an extensive root system, so it spreads quickly and chokes out the other plants in a garden. A weed is a weed.

THREE MONTHS EARLIER

I surprised David with small gifts while I cheated on him with a fellow teacher, a writer who often dropped phrases like *sign as both mark and meaning* into conversation. I let him tease me for dating David, the school's landscaper. The last gift I gave David was a cactus in a miniscule ceramic pot. The gift before that, a Zen garden with a Lilliputian rake. Before that, a dwarf bonsai tree. That all these gifts were miniatures seems a sign of the tightness of my heart back then, the smallness of who I was. Or maybe they signified nothing at all.

A YEAR BEFORE

David helped me start a plot in the community garden, where we planted tomatoes and lettuces. When tiny leaves sprouted, he bent to inspect them, his hands deft as he pressed a leaf between thumb and forefinger. He gave me directions on watering and aeration, but I only half listened, savoring the taste of words like *bonemeal* and *humus.*

That I could grow anything astounded me, though I knew it wouldn't be long before the plot burned out.

THE BEGINNING

David and I ate lunch in the school's garden—raised beds of beans, cucumbers, and squash. He once plucked a fat heirloom tomato from the vine and held it up for careful inspection. Seeds are passed down each season to preserve desirable traits like juiciness or color, he explained, holding up the misshapen tomato, shades of purple and deep orange stretched across its skin. Each variety is genetically unique, and that's what gives them their resistance to pests and diseases. The French sometimes call it *pomme d'amour*, he added, and offered me a taste.

AT THE DOG PARK

At the dog park, I pull in behind a gold SUV with a bumper sticker that reads: "Don't let this fool you, my real treasure is in Heaven." Additional stickers read: "The Spirit Moves Me" and "ReJOYce." I know the woman who drives the car. She tells me her daughters don't like her, but she has many friends at the park and often whips out her cell to load up someone's digits. ReJOYce wears expensive jogging suits, and her dog has its very own quilted down vest with a fashionable collar that turns up. My dog, Oscar, looks at me with his pleading brown Cleopatra eyes when he sees ReJOYce and her yappy Jack Russell, Portia. Oscar is a large, gentle golden retriever, and dogs like Portia make us both nervous: her shrill bark and sprightly dance steps—back and forth and around—forever moving.

I will admit that I sometimes take a turn around the park with ReJOYce. She tells me about making mega-nachos and watching football with her husband. ReJOYce even gives me the recipe for the nachos, and I nod enthusiastically as if I'm going to make them. And then I do make them. I don't watch football, and my husband isn't home, so I eat the nachos right off the tray, standing at my kitchen counter, listening to a story on the radio about a group of kids who, it seems just because they can, leave a man to die in a well.

At the dog park, there is a dog named Satan. He is part shar-pei and part boxer, and he is wrinkled and earnest. Satan, one might say, is eager to please. I often walk the park with Satan's master, who is bearded, large, and very friendly. He borders on gleeful when he introduces his dog to someone new at the park. Sometimes ReJOYce, Satan's master, and I walk together with our dogs. It would be nice if one day Satan's master asked ReJOYce about her real treasure in Heaven, but only so much can happen at the dog park.

* * *

At the dog park, it does sometimes happen that Satan's master, ReJOYce, and I all round the path at the same time with a philosophy professor. We walk together, a loosely tethered pack. The Professor doesn't talk to us much, but when he does, he always gesticulates wildly. Most of the time he texts while he walks. His dog, Heidi—short for Heidegger (of course)—is an affable mutt. After I hear the story about the kids who leave the man at the bottom of a well, I ask the Professor to explain to me how it's possible for people, even children, to do something so horrid. He talks first of compassion and empathy and then about mankind's capacity to find wonder and even pleasure in evil acts. He throws some phrases at me: "The normalization of deviance" is one of them. I want to get more examples of how people find pleasure in evil, and I'd like to get his opinion on whether he thinks my husband might qualify as one of these types of people, but before I get a chance Portia nips Satan, and our group disintegrates.

One day at the dog park, I find my group and amble along the dirt path, watching Oscar swish through the tall grasses. Per usual, it's the Professor, ReJOYce, Satan's

Master, and me. I'd like to say that on this day ReJOYce and the Professor get into an argument about salvation. Unfortunately for me, that never happens. But what does happen, as we are all loping through the park with our sweet dogs, is that in the not-too-far distance, a car spontaneously erupts into flames. Big, tall, Heaven-licking flames. There is smoke, fire, and general chaos as Satan's master and I sprint toward the blaze. My ribs ache from running and probably because they never healed right after being broken. The dogs race ahead of us, their muscled haunches propelling them forward, and even Oscar, with his dysplastic sway of a gait, keeps up with the pack, a trail of dust kicking up in their wake.

In the lot, other dog park people huddle in small groups not far from the car. "What in the fuck happened?" Satan's master yells to no one in particular, and I watch people shrug their shoulders and raise their hands in confusion. "We were walking through the lot, and it was just *boom!* and flames." This from a petite woman whose Rhodesian ridgeback, Tyco (the Psycho), often bodychecks Oscar midstride. I don't blame Tyco for doing it; it's an instinct passed down from his lion-hunting ancestors. Not his fault. The woman keeps repeating her story to anyone who comes on the scene, so I move away from her.

The car is pretty much obliterated, a charred mass pouring out smoke. The air is heavy with fumes, and the scent of exhaust and fuel makes me nauseated. The Professor walks closer to the car, and several yell for him to stay back. "But we need to see if anyone's inside, don't we?" he asks. "Well, they'd be toast," replies Satan's Master, and I give him a look. Sirens blare in the distance, and I know it's a matter of a few minutes before the cavalry arrives. I back away from the flames and watch ReJOYce stride purposefully toward the car, brush past the Professor, and crouch next to what would have been the front seat. "Get away from there," I shout. "You could get hurt!" She ignores me and circles the smoking wreck.

The firefighters and police tell ReJOYce and the rest of us to go back to the park and leave it to them. We follow their orders and begin another circuit of the trail, each of us exclaiming, "How horrible!" "How strange!" We speculate. "More likely than not," says Satan's Master, "the car had some kind of engine malfunction, or some factory defect that made it blow." He nods his head up and down, sure of himself, and I wonder what expertise he has that makes him so confident. "Yeah," concurs ReJOYce, and I'm surprised and disappointed that she doesn't have something more to say. She never says what I think she might, considering the stickers she plasters on her car, and I often feel deceived by her. "Maybe someone made the car explode," I offer.

The Professor looks up from his phone and squints at me: "Why would you say that?"

"Because it happens," I reply.

"Yeah, well, I'm sure that's not what happened here." The Professor starts texting again.

"How do you know?" I ask. It seems as plausible to me that someone blew up the car as it does that the engine malfunctioned.

"Because people don't do things like that unless they're crazy," says Satan's Master. He looks over and gives me a little shrug and neck jut. Duh.

I don't say anything else, but what I'm thinking is that people do things like that all the time even when they're not crazy. Kids leave a terrified man at the bottom of a well to die because they can. A husband breaks his wife's ribs because she's late or breaks her nose because the dog chews up his book. That husband isn't crazy, and I don't think those kids are either. And while I haven't done the following, I can imagine it easily: sinking a silver knife deep into my husband's flesh, just beneath his ribs; or the solid thud of a wooden bat connecting with his skull; or maybe the way his skin would melt and then char if I rigged his car to go *boom* and then up in flames. I'm not crazy, but I could do all these things.

It is only when my husband kicks Oscar's weak leg so hard it pops the dog's hip out of its socket that I leave. I pick up my beautiful boy, who cowers at the edge of the rug, looking at me for an explanation, and I carry him out of the house, my face buried in the fur beside the silky flap of his ear. "I'm sorry, I'm so sorry," I whisper, and Oscar turns his head to try and lick my face.

I don't need anyone to point out the irony of leaving my husband only when he kicked the dog. I know better than to try and explain to my closest friend how it's different, but I do anyway. Yes, I tell my friend, my husband is a monster for breaking my nose and my ribs, but it takes an altogether different kind of beast to kick a dog when he's down. *Literally.* My friend fidgets and looks away. It probably doesn't help that I proffer a stiff *ha-ha-ha.* I know nothing about the situation is funny, but I don't know how else to talk about it. And so, I stop.

* * *

There is a German surgeon visiting the vet program at the state university, and I use part of my savings to buy Oscar a new titanium hip the surgeon has designed and will implant. Oscar will be the first dog in the state with this kind of hip, and I don't bat an eye at the expense. The surgeon's long explanation of why this titanium hip is superior and worth the cost is completely unnecessary. I can't stop thinking of the way Oscar tried to stand up after my husband kicked him, his dislocated leg dragging uselessly beneath him. I keep seeing the stark white x-ray image of his leg—the ball of his femur pointed violently and unnaturally away from its nest of a socket. Ligaments and tendons must tear clean through and the joint capsule must rupture in order to produce an image like the one I saw. It seems only right that Oscar at least gets the best hip on the market.

After his surgery, my bionic boy hobbles along beside me, supported by a towel that I loop under his belly and hold by its handles, which takes some of the weight off his back legs. We are a sight as we shuffle along through our new neighborhood. A six-legged oddity. When we walk, I scan my new neighborhood for my husband's car, a black SUV with one of those embarrassing marathon stickers boasting *26.2* slapped on the rear window. How is it that I chose this man, I often think. He is supposed to stay a hundred yards away from me per the protection order I was granted, but my husband is a bender of rules. He is a man who finds a way to the front of every line without upsetting anyone, who creates a parking space where none exists, who talks his way to a restaurant table that's been booked for months. He is a man who can beat up his wife and be forgiven. "Charming" is what certain people might call him.

During the three months of Oscar's recovery, the dog park is off-limits, and I wonder if he misses Satan and Heidi, possibly even jittery Portia. Since we started going to the dog park a year ago, we've rarely missed our thrice-weekly visits. I even went with my nose still swollen, purple shadows beneath both eyes. When I told the dog park crew that I'd been hit in the face with a fastball at the company picnic, only Satan's master looked at me for a beat too long. I wonder whether any of my dog park friends would spend five grand on a titanium hip for a dog. I decide ReJOYce is the only one who would.

Now, instead of the dog park, Oscar and I drive to the state university twice a week for his physical therapy. He walks on a treadmill in a glass tank of water to build up the muscles in his hindquarters. I don't tell anyone about it. There is only so much most people are willing to swallow when it comes to caring for a pet, and, like a titanium hip, hydrotherapy isn't one of them. Oscar slow-motion canters in the water tank, and the feathered fur on the back of his legs streams behind him like golden seaweed. Though I know it's not possible, I imagine muscles and tendons growing stronger, wrapping around the gleaming titanium of his hip, repairing what's been broken. His leonine head occasionally turns toward me, checking to see that I'm still there, and I call to him, "Keep going, Oscar! That's a good boy!" I clap and yell encouragement like a demented cheerleader.

It's required, in order to avoid dislocation post-surgery, that Oscar be crated at night and anytime I'm not at home. Oscar hasn't spent a day of his life in a crate, and though I know many dogs supposedly find them comforting, I hate the idea of him being in what, let's be frank, is a cage. But I'm told it's a must if Oscar is to heal without incident, so I buy the most gigantic crate I can find, and Oscar still seems crowded in it. He has enough room to lie down and turn around and resettle, but it's like seeing the Siberian tiger at my city's zoo: wrong. I once watched that tiger obsessively pace the quarter-mile perimeter of his cage when he'd naturally roam and hunt in a range of thirty or forty miles. What is he thinking, I still wonder, during the hundreds of caged laps he performs each day. *Is* he thinking? Whatever the circumstances of his being there—born into captivity, rescued from poachers, nursed back to health—does it make a difference if his biology demands he be able to roam?

In our new apartment, I position Oscar's crate by my bed, and we stare at each other for a few minutes before I remove one side of the cage, drag the mattress and comforter off my bed, and sleep on the floor beside him. It goes on like this for a month. Oscar's nose twitches in his sleep, and his legs jerk slightly as he dream-chases a rabbit or squirrel. His sighs are soft and contented, but occasionally, in the deep of night, he emits a strangled squeak or bark in his sleep, so I reach out to him, run my hands through the crest of fur and loose skin at the back of his neck, and tell him, *It's okay, I'm still here.*

Often, in the middle of the night, Oscar whines to go pee, and I have to rig up his towel harness and take him out to my building's front yard. Each time, I'm sure this will be the night I see my husband's car drive past. He doesn't have my new address, but I imagine it wouldn't be hard to get. Just because I've never seen him doesn't mean he hasn't been here. In the landscape of my head, his car glides through the thick darkness of my neighborhood like a two-ton shark. Some nights I dream of how and where he'll show up: I turn the corner of a hallway in my office building, and there he is; I open the door to leave my apartment, and he stands so close I can smell his breath; he stands in the doorway of my childhood bedroom in a house two states away; he comes toward me, the tall grasses in the dog park swirling around his legs.

When I wake from these dreams, I am cold and relieved. He is a man who wouldn't be caught dead in a dog park. "A bastion of bougie weirdos and housewives" is what he called it.

In the summer, Oscar gets the okay to return to the dog park. I scan the fields for Tyco the Psycho before we enter, worried that his signature body check might be too much for Oscar's hip, bionic though it may be. I cringe at the thought of his slick titanium femoral head slipping from the curve of his radiant new acetabulum. But, as soon as I open the gate, Oscar makes a break for the prairie grass, his sickled tail waving its goodbye. I find him with our group among the Indian grass and bluestem at the far end of the park, and they call out their *Hellos!* and *Where have you beens?* The Professor even pauses from texting. "I was so worried Oscar had died." The way he throws his arms out from his sides, shaking his hands spastically, is oddly soothing to me. ReJOYce wants every detail of Oscar's surgery and recuperation and is duly impressed that Oscar runs on the only titanium hip in the state. "I would have done the same for Portia," she tells me, and I am triumphant that I've predicted ReJOYce would say this.

Satan's master gets down on his knees and holds Oscar's head, letting the dog's long pink tongue lap at the bare skin above his beard, and I regret not congratulating him the day we found out the car explosion was just an engine malfunction—that he'd been right after all. I feel my chest tighten, and a tingling ache spreads through my thoracic cavity and tunnels up my throat. For a moment, it's as if I'm underwater. I feel the slight, almost soft, resistance against my body, and then we begin to walk. I describe Oscar's hydrotherapy in detail, and they have many questions about how he negotiated being crated. When I tell them I caved and slept on the floor beside Oscar, Satan's master responds, "What other choice did you have?"

* * *

My lawyer tells me my divorce will settle quickly. I'm not asking for anything, so there's nothing for my husband to fight me over. While I wait for the divorce to go through, my husband never shows up at my job to harass me. He never pounds on my door in the dead of night, threatening me or pleading with me for forgiveness. He never corners me in the parking lot of my apartment building or follows me home from work. He never does what I imagine or dream he might do while we wait in marital purgatory.

Until one day he does. The day after our divorce is finalized, my ex-husband shows up at the dog park. We are circling the back loop when Satan's master points and remarks, "Who comes to the dog park in a blazer? What a douche nozzle." I look up to see him about fifty yards out, striding purposefully toward us in crisp, dark jeans and a gray blazer. There's no denying that he's an attractive man—lean, long-legged, and classically handsome. If he were a dog, he'd be a Weimaraner: alert, athletic, and bred to hunt. "Which dog is his?" asks ReJOYce. He's getting closer to us, and I call out for Oscar, who comes bounding to my side. "Well," I say, "once Oscar was his dog. I mean we shared him." The Professor looks up from his phone and glances at my ex, who's closing in. "He shouldn't be wearing such nice shoes in a dog park," the Professor remarks.

I hear a buzzing noise, and I'm not sure if it's inside or outside my head. There is so much to tell these people in the minutes before my ex is upon us. There is one story that they're telling themselves about him as he approaches, and then there is the story I could tell them. But all I can say is, "He can't take Oscar. He cannot take my dog." I repeat this again and again, and I can see that ReJOYce is alarmed. She stares at me, blinking rapidly. Satan is circling us, chasing after Portia, and Oscar leans against my thigh. Heidi, the Professor's dog, starts barking, as if she knows my ex doesn't belong. The ringing in my ears gets stronger, and I feel a pulsing ache in my head, like I'm upside down and all the blood in my body is rushing to my skull, filling my sinuses, the sockets behind my eyes, any pocket of space in my cranium.

"He won't take Oscar." I think it's ReJOYce who says this, but the voice sounds muted, like I have water in my ears. "He hurt Oscar," I blurt out. The Professor puts his phone in his pocket, and ReJOYce stops staring at me and turns to face my ex-husband, who is now just feet from us. Oscar whines, and Satan's master starts walking toward my ex, ReJOYce on his heels. "My nose that time," I say, and Satan's master, ReJOYce, and the Professor all stop to look at me. "He did that to me." It's such a simple thing to say, I think. And then they are upon him.

THEN GO TO PARIS, I SAY

My mother is beautiful even when she bangs her head against the wall. When she does, her black, shiny hair swings back and forth, and I can see in profile the swell of her upper lip hanging just a bit over the lower one. Thin blue veins strain up and down her slender neck. My father—when he tells the story of meeting her—says she was a stone-cold fox.

We are eating dinner in the breakfast room, the four of us kids and my mother. I'm particularly pleased because she's served us spaghetti in the bowls from France that have a little painted boy or girl on the bottom and small flat handles on each side. Guessing whether we have a girl or boy at the bottom of our bowl is a favorite game.

Boy, my older sister guesses. *Girl*, says my brother. *Girl*, from my little sister who has yet to eat a bite of food. They wait for my guess, but I'm in the middle of counting the number of noodles I've eaten and am afraid if I pause, I may lose count, and, well, then it's all over. *Come on*, they say, *guess already*. *Boy*, I mumble, trying to hold on to the number seventeen in my head, but my younger sister Margot starts in with the moaning—her nightly ritual—and I know that things will only go downhill from here.

Margot clutches her stomach and continues to groan and claim that she feels like she's being stabbed. She is six years old but looks about four because she barely eats. My parents have taken her to doctors, specialists even, but nothing's ever been found to be wrong with her. She knocks her bowl away from her, and rice with cinnamon, raisins, and butter—the only meal she'll eat—spills across the table. The raisins look like a trail of slugs inching toward me, and I can't remember how many noodles I've eaten.

My mother, who is in the kitchen making dessert—fresh fruit and cottage cheese—screams at Margot to eat her food. I plot the ways I can make myself a new bowl of spaghetti, start my count over, and get it right this time. If I don't, something very bad will happen. Take your pick: Margot will die of starvation, my brother Max will get hit by a car, Elyse will be kidnapped, or my father will die in a plane crash.

Margot is still whimpering when my mother brings us the fruit and cottage cheese. My mother doesn't believe in serving processed foods or sugary desserts. She won't use a microwave and cooks bulgur wheat, quinoa, and steel-cut oats long before they become trendy. All we want is some Magic Shell or Cap'n Crunch like the rest of America. I am pretty sure that Margot's stomach hurts because any time my mother isn't in the kitchen, Margot climbs up on the counter to get to the sugar, used only for my father's coffee, and hoovers as much as she can before she hears someone coming.

Margot, the most daring of us all, continues to groan, and when my mother sets the fruit and cottage cheese before her, Margot shoves it as hard as she can, and the curds and cubed pears fly everywhere. Max and Elyse shovel down their dessert and clear their places, and I could do the same, except that if I do, I know someone will die tonight. It's imperative that I start over with the spaghetti and count every noodle I swallow until my bowl is empty, and I can see a little French girl or boy grinning up at me.

My mother looks at the cottage cheese, rice, raisins, and pears splattered across our kitchen table, and a low moan rises from her throat. She turns toward the closest wall and begins to knock her forehead against it, lightly at first but then harder and faster. *You kids*, she says. *Just wait until I leave you and go to Paris. I will. I will go to Paris to live with my sisters and leave you all here with your father.* She is crying now and continues to beat her forehead against the wall. There is a rhythm to it: Bang, *Paris.* Bang, *I will leave you.* Bang, *get on a plane.* Bang, *gone.*

Elyse and Max watch from the kitchen for a few seconds and then go upstairs to their rooms. Margot has left the table and is picking through the bag of raisins on the kitchen counter. But I stay at the table, unable to look away from my mother. Her hair swishes this way and that, and snot drips from her nose over those full, raspberry lips. I watch my mother as she knocks her head against the wall, and I count: fourteen knocks, nine *Paris*es, seven *I will leave you*s. I am more unnerved by the odd number of *Paris*es and *I will leave you*s than by what she is doing or saying.

That night, it takes so long for the house to go dark and quiet. My father arrives home from work late, after we are all in bed. I hear murmuring from my parents' room, and I wait. Finally, when everyone is asleep, I sneak down to the kitchen and get the leftover spaghetti out of the refrigerator. I take one of the bowls from France and look at the grinning girl peering out from inside before I fill it. I count each noodle as it goes down my throat: twenty-one, twenty-two, twenty-three. Our house is old, and I hear the creaks and groans as it settles in the night. The spaghetti is cold, and the noodles are hard to swallow. *Then go to Paris,* I say between bites and numbers. *Then go to Paris,* I say.

FIVE THINGS YOU SHOULD KNOW ABOUT NUMBER FIVE

1.

She is called Number Five because she is the fifth child of twelve, and lest you think this is sad or somehow neglectful, know that it is not uncommon in Vietnamese culture to call people by their birth order number like a nickname. Five is the smartest of the children, which means she earns the most rides in her father's American convertible. Her father, a doctor, drives the only Chevy Bel Air convertible in all of Phnom Penh, where he moved from Vietnam long before she was born. As she drives through the city with him, the wind whips her black hair around her face, and Five pretends she is in the movies, that James Dean is driving her to a beach where they'll spread a blanket and watch surfers crest crashing swells. James will offer her a cigarette, and she'll inhale expertly, exhale perfect rings that float above them toward the clouds. Five's fingers twitch slightly, maneuvering the imaginary cigarette as her father's convertible floats like a barge toward his club, where she always orders Coca-Cola and french fries. Five loves all things American—the movies, the food, the jeans, the language, and the men who she believes are all lean and blue-eyed like James Dean.

2.

Number Five leaves Cambodia to study in Europe. She says goodbye to the beautiful white house she's lived in all her life. Goodbye to the enormous silk cotton tree that looms over the back garden. Goodbye to the cook who always sneaks the children a spoonful of condensed milk before bed. Five says goodbye to her girlfriends and promises to write them even though she's grown tired of them and is ready to move on. Goodbye to her siblings who are still young enough to be at home. Numbers Six through

Twelve line the driveway like the palm trees whose massive green fronds sway overhead. She hugs each of them, and when she gets to Number Twelve, who is only nine, she holds him for a beat longer than the rest and slips chocolate wrapped in gold foil into his small hand. Finally, she says goodbye to her parents. Her father beams, his wide grin both joyful and proud. Her mother lightly taps her fisted hands against the sides of her legs, something she does when she's nervous.

3.

Five will not see her parents for almost a decade. In that time, she will finish with university and fall in love with an American man who is lean, blue eyed, and studying in Madrid at the same time as her. She will follow her James Dean to America where, no matter her story, people will assume she's a war bride. Five and her James Dean will eventually move to a suburb of a large city where their neighbors will cross the street when they see her strolling the neighborhood with her husband after dinner. The next time Five sees her parents, they will have lost everything:

their home, her father's practice, their country. But worst of all, they will have lost two of her brothers to the war, Numbers Six and Seven, who loved to hide in the massive branches of the cotton silk tree when it was time for homework, whose laughter Five can still hear echoing from the treetop. The next time Five sees her parents, they will be in a one-room apartment outside of Paris, the last stop after they walked for days through a jungle in order to be loaded onto a plane and flown to a country that had colonized their own so many years before.

4.

When the neighbor's daughter spits on one of Five's daughters and calls her a dirty chink, Five and her husband move the family to a different suburb where people don't use racial slurs but continually mistake Five for her children's nanny, looking past her in stores and addressing her eldest daughter as if she is in charge. During the day, Five takes care of her children. She cuts vegetables for dinner, sweeps the floors. She reads to the youngest two and then falls asleep with them during nap time, dreams she is eating rambutan with her sisters in the garden behind her childhood home. The juice runs over her fingers and drips down her chin. The fruit is so sweet, her sisters' chatter so sharp that when Five wakes up, it takes her a minute to realize where she is and that her youngest child has wet the bed.

5.

Five will never go back to Cambodia or Vietnam, though she has the chance. *There is nothing left for me there,* she tells her husband. Instead, she takes her children to visit her parents in their tiny apartment outside of Paris, the apartment they live in until they die. When they are young, her children sleep there on small cots, borrowed from one of Five's sisters who lives nearby. Five sets up the children's cots between their grandparents' twin beds and sets up her own in the narrow kitchen. Her mother burns incense on a small altar with the few pictures she still has of Six and Seven and leaves a mango on the altar until its musky flesh rots. Five's father bends over his desk, cramped at the foot of his bed, and examines a map of Asia, traces his finger across the page. Five's children complain about the smallness of the apartment, their boredom. She looks into their brown eyes so similar to her own but sees nothing else of herself in them. In three weeks, she will fly back to the States with her kids, back to her husband, back to their house in the suburbs where nobody looks like her. Flying above the ocean, her children finally asleep beside her, Five will look out the window, think about all the places she has left in the world, and consider the strange comfort of hurling hundreds of miles per hour so high above the earth.

BEGGARS' NIGHT

She arrives on my porch on Beggars' Night, without a costume, and it takes me a minute to place her. Children scream and careen through my neighborhood dressed as zombies and ninjas. Grim executioners and glittering fairies pound and flit across lawns in search of sugar. Behind her, I see a skinny monster lurching up my driveway. I quickly turn off my porch light, signaling our house is closed for business, and Frankenstein veers toward the house next door.

The woman on my porch leans into the screen door, her face illuminated by the plastic skull lights staked in our window box. She is grinning, and her eyes are bright. I can feel the sweat trickle down one side of my ribs, and I wonder how long my daughter and husband will be.

"So do you think we should talk?" She is somehow still grinning while she asks me this, her face a mask of happiness and goodwill. The woman opens the screen door without waiting for me to reply, and I just barely have time to step back before she's in my living room. "I think we should talk," she says. "I don't know that I want to do that—" I start to tell her, but she just keeps talking over me. "Yes, I think we should all get together and have a big group talk." She is still smiling.

The woman is looking at the painting behind me, and she walks past me, closer to it. "We're splitting up, you know." She's still staring at the painting, and I don't know if I should reply.

"I'm really sorry," I say to her. "I didn't mean for this to happen." But it doesn't seem as if she's heard me, or more likely she doesn't care if I'm sorry. One of my daughter's plastic swords sits on the bench below the painting, and the woman bends to pick it up. Mia is out in the neighborhood dressed as a knight. Her insistence on swords and bows and arrows over crowns and wands is a secret source of pride. This evening, she'd even insisted I use goopy fake blood to paint battle wounds across her cheeks and forehead. The woman runs her hands over the toy sword and drops it back onto the bench with a clatter. *Ha* is all she says.

She walks past me, deeper into the house, and I follow her, as if she's the one who lives here and is giving me a tour. I hear dogs barking and the high-pitched screams of children hopped up on candy and being out past dark. I know as I follow her that I should demand she get the hell out of my house, but instead I feel my teeth clack and chatter against each other, and I can't make them stop. The woman is in the playroom now, and she's taking a photo off the wall. It's a picture I took of Mia as a toddler, her eyes opened wide in fear and excitement as she slips down a slide at the park. At the bottom edge of the photo is my husband, crouched below the mouth of the slide, his back to the camera.

The woman looks up at me from the picture, that grin of hers still plastered across her face. Her hands are shaking, and I can hear the rattle of glass against the wooden frame. Her long, blond hair swings to and fro as she looks back down at the picture then up at me, again and again. Her eyes finally rest on me, waiting. I think of everything that's before me, of what I'll have to tell my husband, and I trip forward, reaching for the photo. There is fake blood caked beneath some of my fingernails, and I think, as I grab for the picture frame, about how hard I will have to scrub to get it out.

SNOW

Though we washed her with wine and rubbed her with butter and garnished her with all the trappings of success, she would not comply. We gave her everything: the white pony on her sixth birthday; the diamond studs on her twelfth; the apple-red convertible for her sixteenth; Grandmother's pearl choker, like so many rows of teeth, for her twenty-first; and then, at twenty-five, she still would not settle down. First, we said it was a stage, a small rebellion before she acquiesced, but that was years ago, and still she insisted it was her choice to marry or not, as if she were some kind of bohemian.

The first man she brought home was the one with the bun, that greasy topknot of hair sitting up there all through Thanksgiving dinner. Next came the one with holes in his ears so large they'd fit the saucers from the Italian bone china tea set we'd gifted her when she was younger. Number three still gives us shivers when we think of the trails of tattoos up and down his arms—snakes, ivy, skulls, and blood drops covering his shoulders and back, creeping around his sides to blanket his chest. When he took off his shirt by the pool, we all gasped in unison. It was her younger brother who yelled, *Rad tats!* and who shook with glee whenever she brought a new man home to visit. We all knew the little brother was a lost cause. It was her we'd pinned our hopes on.

The fourth one seemed normal at first, but a few minutes into dinner he shared that he was raised in Florida, and we all choked on our soup just a little. The fifth man came in a midi-skirt that matched hers, his calf muscles bulging obscenely below its hem. When he discussed feminist theory at dinner, Grandmother fell asleep before the first course was cleared. The sixth was Canadian, and we have nothing more to say about that. The seventh came to us with flowers and chocolates, but the flowers were carnations, and the chocolates were chalky, and when he spoke of the Iowan cornfields behind his family's farmhouse, we imagined the stink of pigs and wrinkled our noses.

Then she came to us alone, a small tattoo of a crown visible above her ankle, a twinkling silver hoop through her nostril, gripping copies of *A Vindication of the Rights of Woman* and *Bad Feminist.* We took in the cutoff shorts and flannel shirt. She looked like a deranged but very beautiful farmer. We tried to listen to what she was saying, we did, but all we could do was stare at the movement of her rose-red lips, her skin like a fine layer of snow, that slim waist, those ankles as narrow and delicate as a bird's rib cage, and her glossy black hair that swung loose as she talked and talked and talked. What she said we could not tell you.

THE DE FACTO MOTHER

Kiki learns that male alligators have permanent erections while she watches the Discovery Channel instead of grading five-paragraph essays from her eighth graders who, among the boys, she also suspects have permanent erections. Over the many years she's taught, she's seen hundreds of boys adjust themselves, eyes darting around the room checking to see if anyone noticed, or openly, without a hint of embarrassment. She has also on occasion watched a boy walk out of her classroom with a full-on tent and the mother in her has wanted to rush over and hand him a folder or a book to cover himself. Which, of course, she resists. Kiki should turn off the television and grade, but she just can't bring herself to read another essay about *The Hate You Give*, a book she and her students love. Reading and discussing books with her students brings Kiki actual joy. Reading their writing is another beast altogether.

During mating, two flatworms, which Kiki has never heard of, engage in "penis fencing," in which they each try to stab each other with their two-headed penises. Yes, this is alarming and surprising to Kiki, but what really gets her is the way the Discovery Channel describes what comes next, which is that whoever manages to penetrate first and inseminate the other *wins*. And the *loser*—their words, not hers—becomes the de facto mother. Kiki considers the flatworm's hermaphroditic nature, what it might be like to have a penis alongside her vagina. Not interested. While she's had her share of penises inside of her, sleeps beside a human with a penis, and has a child with a penis, she will always find them strange and somewhat ugly. She realizes that if a man described a vagina this way, it would be viewed as misogynistic. Maybe she's biased, but vaginas just seem more organic to the human body.

Kiki glances at the stack of essays beside her on the couch and feels slightly nauseated. She tells herself that it's because there's eighty of them, but also, her period is a couple of weeks late, and she's been putting off buying a pregnancy test. Kiki loves her son, but she is not interested in having another baby—she hated being pregnant, and she's only ever wanted a single child. Lucas, her husband, is another story. "Two is perfect," he keeps telling her. "Then they have each other." Kiki won't budge—even when they were dating, she made it clear that *if* she had children, it would only be one. Anders is four, a sweet, gentle little boy who loves animals and has the palate of an adult. She loves him more than anything in the world, which is why she only ever wanted one child. How could she possibly love another child as much as she loves Anders?

On television, a hen squawks and does its strange head-bobbing run across a farmyard, a fat rooster in hot pursuit. Kiki watches as the rooster, who, just for the record, seems both predatory and peremptory, mounts the hen. She knows she's anthropomorphizing, and the rooster is just following his biological urges, but watching him mount that hen makes her mad. Some of that anger dissipates when the Aussie host of the show shares that a hen can eject up to eighty percent of an *offending* (again, their words, not hers) male's sperm. She silently cheers on the hen: *eject, eject, eject!* Once again, the Discovery Channel disappoints when it underscores that this ejection of sperm allows for the possibility that the hen might be impregnated by a rooster at the top of the pecking order. Is it so impossible that a hen just doesn't want to get impregnated yet again? The TV host did, after all, describe hens who eject sperm as *enraged* or possibly *disappointed.* Why assume she's disappointed the rooster isn't distinguished enough—too low in the pecking order? Why not focus on the possibility that the hen is enraged at the rooster's audacity, at the prospect of laying another bunch of eggs, with the idea of being, yet again, an incubator?

Kiki clicks off the television and puts aside her stack of essays. She slings her purse over her shoulder and grabs her keys. At the pharmacy down the street, she selects two pregnancy tests. Sitting awkwardly on the toilet, trying to pee on the stick but not her hand—harder than it might sound—Kiki thinks about the flatworms, wonders if her husband would be so gung ho about two kids if he *lost* their battle and became the de facto mother.

TRIMMED

The woman notices during her bikini wax that she's stopped feeling any pain—completely—not even the tiniest flash of it. The blue strip of gummy wax the aesthetician rips off after a quick *one, two, three* warning is covered in hair, but the searing ache and burn she's always felt, no matter how many waxes she's had, is gone. *None, nada, niente.* She doesn't even flinch. The woman tells the esthetician to keep going—"Gimme a Brazilian! Take it all off!" she shouts gleefully. When the esthetician tells the woman to flip over to kneeling, so she can really get in those crevices, the woman turns over enthusiastically. In that position, leaning on her elbows and forearms, butt high in the air, she imagines she's poised to take off in a race, albeit a rather strange one.

At home, she strips naked in front of the full-length mirror in her bedroom. She runs her hand over the smooth baldness of her genitalia, bends this way and that to examine other parts of herself. Her arms, which haven't ever struck the woman as particularly hirsute, suddenly seem apelike in comparison to her smooth legs and her now very smooth crotch. She goes to the bathroom and shaves off all her arm hair. The hair makes a small wispy nest around the drain of the sink. In the reflection of her medicine cabinet mirror, the woman's head now seems monstrously hairy—Medusa with a head full of hair snakes. She gathers her dark brown mane into a ponytail, snips the long whip of hair at the base of the tail, and tosses it into the sink. The electric razor vibrates over her scalp as she zips it front to back again and again. The dark nest of hair in her sink grows big enough to house several large birds.

The woman nicks herself badly on the last pass over her skull, and although she can see a bloom of red spread above her right ear, once again she doesn't feel even the slightest twinge of pain. She presses small pieces of damp toilet paper to the cut—a trick she learned from a friend when she first began to shave her legs in middle school. The paper sticks and soaks up some of the blood that continues to seep out. But for the sodden pieces of toilet paper glued above her ear, her scalp is now a glossy beautiful dome. Not a hair in sight. Her brows, however, look atrocious, like tarantulas creeping across her forehead, so she shaves them off too.

In front of the full-length mirror in her bedroom, the woman marvels at her polished, hairless self. She is meeting friends that night, so she selects a sleek pair of black leather pants that taper at the ankle and a cropped black sweater to match. She eyes a new pair of four-inch black stiletto ankle boots on the rack in her closet and nods her head yes, yes, yes! When the woman slides on the leather pants and steps back to examine herself, she sees that the leather strains out a bit at the top of her inner thighs—small but noticeable bulges where the pants should lie smooth. She walks toward the mirror to get a closer look, and she can hear the swishing of her leather-clad thighs against one another. Not a problem, she thinks, and goes to the hall closet to grab the toolbox her father gave her when she moved into her first apartment.

The woman plucks a square of sandpaper from the toolbox and congratulates herself on her stellar solution to the thigh problem. But her satisfaction vanishes, and she's seized with fear: What if there are limits to her newfound painlessness? What if her luck has run out? She fetches the razor blade she keeps to scrape burned food off her stovetop, pulls down her pants, pinches some of the meat of her inner left thigh and etches a small line—not even a smidgen of pain.

Convinced that pain has left her permanently, the woman begins to sand the inside of her thighs, just up high where she'd prefer they didn't meet. She whistles a happy tune as she sands away and remembers how her father used to whistle while sanding the birdhouses he made. She watches her skin come off in specks like dust motes floating in the light and feels nothing. Impatient to get the job done, she applies more pressure so that peels of skin slide off. She smiles at the neatness of how her skin peels, takes pleasure in the process in the same way she finds peeling a cucumber pleasurable—how the deep green skin unravels so easily from the flesh of the vegetable. Sure, there's some blood, but her tight leather pants will take care of that.

In front of her full-length mirror, the woman admires how her pants cling just right to the inside of her thighs. She presses her legs together, and they only meet at her bony knees—the backdrop of her sunny bedroom reflects perfectly through the distinctive gap in her mirrored thighs. She pulls the soft, cropped sweater over her head and steps back to assess the effect, at which point she notices a small layer of fat that pops just the slightest bit over the waist of her pants. That absolutely won't do, she thinks, and goes to the kitchen for the scissors she uses to cut pizza, clothing tags, stringy meat, you name it. Knowing she won't feel a thing, she begins to trim with abandon. A snip of skin here, a snip of skin there, until there isn't a hint of that sad little mushroom cap of fat, and the waist of her leather pants rests seamlessly on her hips. While the woman doesn't feel any pain, there is quite a lot of blood. Not to worry, the woman thinks and wraps her waist in layer after layer of toilet paper. "Best trick ever," she says to herself and thinks fondly of her old pal Beth from middle school.

The woman takes in her reflection: her shiny smooth skin and chic attire. She edits out the reams of toilet paper as she'll be sure to remove those before she leaves the apartment. Her new silky suede boots are the pièce de résistance, and she sits to put them on. The towering stiletto heel makes for a violently arched shank, and the woman strains mightily as she tries to angle her feet down into the ankle boots. After a few minutes, she crouches on the floor of her bedroom, peers into the toolbox, and finds the hammer she uses to hang framed photos. She pounds first her left foot, then her right, smashing all the bones with zeal. The woman marvels, for the fourth time that day, that nothing, not a single thing she does to her body, hurts anymore. She swings away until the broken bones in her feet feel like marbles beneath her fingertips, and then she mashes a foot into each of her glorious boots. When she tries to stand up, the woman falls over immediately, but crawling isn't a problem, and as she crawls toward the mirror in her elegant all-black ensemble, blood dripping through the toilet paper around her waist, a trickle of red seeping down from her glossy skull, she feels like some kind of lithe, bald panther, a sleek, swift, hairless puma. She feels so beautiful she could die.

A GOOK, NOT A CHINK

The boys are in the car parked under a bridge, waiting for their fathers to come out of the bar. The moon, almost perfectly full, hangs low, and under its yellow glow, Nitz sketches pictures of machine guns and Glocks. His Korean mother can't say *th* and pronounces her son's name *Ken-nitz.* Max christened him Nitz when they were little kids, and now everyone but Nitz's family uses the nickname. Max is thankful his Vietnamese mother's English is close to fluent, just the trace of an untraceable accent.

The boys' fathers are both white, but somehow in Max's family it's like the white blots out the Vietnamese, whereas in Nitz's the white is just a background on which to paint his mother's Korean-ness. This goes against Max's mom's theory that when an Asian marries "a white," the Asian overpowers the white only if the man is Asian. Max has explained to his mother that this sounds like a pretty sexist theory.

Max is jealous of his friend's artistic skill. Nitz's drawings are meticulous, the trigger of the Glock angled just right, the safety leaned up against it like a smaller, more cautious brother. The molded dotting on the pistol grip is so precise that Max can almost feel the soft bite of the handle against his bare palm. The drawing has taken Nitz only about fifteen minutes to complete, but now he's already bored, jiggling his leg and flicking his pencil against the window. He grabs his backpack, and Max hears the flat clang of his spray paint cans.

"Come on, let's go up on the bridge."

"We're supposed to stay in the car."

"Then stay."

Max watches Nitz climb the embankment up to the bridge and, after just a minute, scrambles after him. He is nearly a year older than Nitz but always follows, always feels younger. At the top of the bridge, Nitz shakes up his cans and with a few graceful arcs and swipes lays down his signature tag: a split-open skull with brains erupting forth like lava. Max breathes in deeply; he loves the chemical scent of the paint, the metallic rattle of the cans as Nitz shakes and reloads. Max only ever watches.

Their fathers know better than to stay in the bar for longer than an hour, but the coolness of the wind at the top of the bridge and the glassy sound of the water on the rocks below make Max hope they stay longer even if it means the wrath of his mother when he gets home. Nitz takes a break from his tagging and leans against the railing, arching his back over the rail as if to survey the sky above.

"Today in algebra, Mike Brimmer asked if my dad ordered my mom from a catalog, and I told him, 'Of course he did; isn't that how everyone gets their wives?'" Nitz offers this news up to Max matter-of-factly, a habit of his that both impresses and annoys Max. He seethes on the inside, not just at the insult but also at Nitz's calm. His friend's candor and seeming bemusement is something Max will never understand.

"Why do you even respond to that shit, Nitz?"

"Someone's got to remind Brimmer he's dumb as fuck."

It's not often that Max gets targeted by a kid like Mike. He likes to think it's because he knows how to fit in, how to like the same things as everyone else. He doesn't bring chả giò in his lunch, or kimchi like Nitz did the other day. The smell of the fermented cabbage had cleared their cafeteria table in less than a minute. Max tells himself that what he does is fit in, something Nitz can't or won't do. But Max knows, really, that he's simply invisible to the boys who give Nitz a hard time. He knows that his meekness is what keeps him safe, and though he's never verbalized any of this, it's also how he knows that Nitz is brave.

"Responding to an idiot like Mike just makes it worse for you."

"Worse how?"

"Just makes it easier for them to pick on you when you act like you care."

"Yeah, well, it shut him up. And pretending not to hear someone call you a chink doesn't mean you don't care, Max. I mean you should've at least told him you're a gook, not a chink."

Nitz laughs, but Max knows he's not joking, that Nitz is trying to embarrass him. And this doesn't even make Max mad, just more ashamed of that day in gym when he struck out, and Henry Scholl, more Neanderthal than human, had walked by him and called over his shoulder with a smile, *Learn how to hit a ball, chink*, the tone and incantation of his insult more on par with *Better luck next time, bro*, like they were friends or something. Max had frozen in that moment. He may have even smiled. When he thinks of it now, he wants to bang his head against the railing of the bridge. Again, and again.

But instead, he pushes Nitz as hard as he can. Max wants to flip him over the railing into the river below for bringing up what he'd told only Nitz. After school that day, full of attitude, he'd replayed the episode with Henry Scholl for Nitz. I should've nailed that giant head of his with my bat, should've told him to go fuck his mother. I should've said, I'm a gook, not a chink, you fucking imbecile. That Nitz has used Max's own words against him makes his stomach burn, his throat ache. That his fear and shame is so easily detectable leaves Max breathless.

GUIDANCE COUNSELING

Lucinda is a high school junior who wears short A-line skirts, ripped fishnet stockings, and combat boots. She's someone Sothea would have been afraid of in high school—back when that look was favored by punks and outcasts. But Sothea isn't in high school; she's Lucinda's high school guidance counselor, and she's meeting with Lucinda to discuss options for college. "I want to make things," Lucinda tells Sothea. The young woman, a girl really, twists her hands on her wrists, wiggles her long slender fingers, pantomiming sewing or maybe woodworking. Sothea is not sure. "I made a shirt in Design II last week, and Ms. Blythe said it's the best one in all three sections." Lucinda is beaming, her thick cat's-eye liner crinkling at the edges. Sothea should have remembered

Lucinda loved fashion design, given that she's been her counselor since Lucinda's first year of high school. But Sothea is extremely tired, and for the last year she's let her work slide.

Lucinda is not a rebel or a punk—the way she dresses is how many of the girls at the high school dress. In fact, Sothea is reminded, as she skims Lucinda's file, that she is the president of the junior class, a starting forward on the soccer team, and in all accelerated courses. "I figure I want to go to Parsons. You know? In NYC?" Sothea tries not to be annoyed by Lucinda's assumption that she wouldn't know Parsons or where it's located. Lucinda is just a girl excited by her prospects, thrilled by the life she imagines unfurling out in front of her like a plush carpet.

Sothea remembers being seventeen, feeling all that possibility laid out before her. Did she dream of becoming a high school guidance counselor? Of course not. But that's where she's found herself at thirty-six. She'd met her husband, a physics teacher at the high school, and now they have a ten-month-old daughter who might very well attend this same school in the distant future. Even though Sothea realizes everyone with small children is exhausted, she wonders how she can already be *this* tired. She watches Lucinda bounce up and down in her chair as she discusses her future. "I want to apprentice with someone big, and I figure Parsons will give me that sort of networking base." Sothea feels an intense desire to lay her head down on her desk and go to sleep.

"Eventually, I want to be the fashion director of a major house." Sothea nods her head, tries to listen. When she was Lucinda's age, Sothea had written in her journal obsessively. Poem after poem after poem. She'd dreamed of becoming a famous poet, and then she'd grown up. "Then I want to create my own label." Lucinda goes on with her list of wants, dreams, and desires, and Sothea continues to nod with as much enthusiasm as she can muster.

During a period of postpartum depression—not blues, nothing like the blues—just a few months after the birth of her daughter, Sothea's husband bought her a dream journal. *Start with this,* he'd encouraged her. *It's just writing down what you dreamed; maybe it'll spark something for you.* She had smiled weakly, and because he was trying so hard, she told him she loved the idea. The journal is teal blue, fat clouds float across the cover, and *dreams* is written in a frilly font—the sort of thing she would never choose for herself—and it sits in the drawer of her bedside table. Occasionally, Sothea pulls out the journal when she wakes up. She smooths her hand over the cover, opens to the first blank page, and sometimes even uncaps a pen, but Sothea never remembers what she dreams.

"Do you think so, Mrs. Johnson?"

Sothea doesn't even try to pretend she was listening. "I'm sorry, Lucinda. Do I think what?"

"Do you think I'll be able to do all of this?" Lucinda's face is so bright, so earnest and excited.

"I once thought I would be a famous poet." Sothea sits back in her ergonomic chair and looks across the desk at the girl. She is surprised by how little shame she feels at her desire to deflate the girl's ambition. Lucinda nods her head *okay* and looks confused before her face darkens and she frowns at Sothea. She stands up and quickly walks toward the door but not before turning to tell her guidance counselor, "Well, maybe the difference between you and me is—" and here the girl pauses and casts her eyes around Sothea's office, with its piles of books and papers, her desk covered in coffee mug stains—"I won't give up."

The girl hovers in the office doorway, as if waiting for Sothea to react.

Sothea doesn't feel the sting Lucinda hoped to deliver; rather she feels proud of the girl's stubborn refusal to foresee any kind of difficulty, let alone failure. Lucinda looks angry but also hurt, and Sothea wants to get up and hug her. Not because she regrets what she said, or feels motherly toward the young woman, but because Sothea wants to latch on to whatever it is that animates the girl. Absorb her up. Suck her dry.

NIGHT

That night we are jumping on the twin beds in our room. Everything is flowers—flowers climbing up the wallpaper, creeping over our bedspreads. We hear our mother call us to come and say goodbye to our father. My parents' room is dim, and my father is on his side in bed, covers pulled up over his shoulders, his head bent in toward his chest, as if he's asleep. It's time to say goodbye, our mother tells us. When I lean in to kiss him on the cheek, I feel his whiskers on my lips. He doesn't move. Afterward, Margot and I sit on our beds and run our toes through the green shag carpeting.

* * *

At night, I dream of climbing things: a sand dune, a hill, a whale that's been beached. I keep trying to get to the top. I dig in with my hands, my knees, my feet, but I keep sliding backward. When I slip down the enormous side of the whale, its skin feels bumpy against my cheek, my lips, and when I claw at the dead animal's skin, it peels off in my hands.

* * *

At night, Margot and I push our twin beds together to make one big bed. We are afraid of everything: the closet, the branch that scratches the window, the creaks of our old house. I remember my father sitting at the foot of my bed. Once I watched him army crawl out of our room and down the hallway. His body slid across the wood lit dimly by a candle-shaped nightlight. When my sister stops responding to my questions, when her breathing changes, and I know she's asleep, I push the closet doors tighter, I touch the window eight times, I reach out to feel my sister's cheek, which is soft like silk, I creep down the hallway to look in my mother's room. A slice of light from the moon cuts across her shiny black hair. Her body makes a hump in the covers.

* * *

Lately I feel like my legs won't work, like they're both numb and ticklish at the same time. I fall on the grass on the way to the car, and my mother yells at me to hurry up. She is always telling me to hurry. To look where I'm going. To get my head out of the clouds. *Focus, Lily. Focus on what's in the front.* What she means to say is *Focus on what's in front of you,* but my mother messes up these phrases. *Run like a chicken with its head off* instead of *like a chicken with its head cut off.* I try to tell her my legs feel funny, but she tells me to stop making up stories and get up off the grass. *It's not the science of rockets, Lily! Walk!* At night, I tell Margot that I might be going cripple, and she tells me to stop acting weird. When her breathing starts to change, and I know she's almost asleep, I tell her that one day we'll both have kids, and our father will never meet them. I hope this keeps her awake. My legs feel like they are full of buzzing bees. I rub my feet together beneath the blankets, try to make the buzzing stop.

* * *

I stand over my mother's bed and watch her sleep. Her eyelids twitch, and the bedcovers rise and fall with her breaths. Her face cream smells like lavender. I poke her lightly on the shoulder, and she turns over, her back curled away from me. I whisper the Our Father at my mother's back eight times. On my father's side of the bed, the sheets feel cool beneath my hand. I take his pillow to my room and rub my bottom lip against the soft, worn case. My legs buzz and ache. I do not want to dream of hills or dead whales, so I listen for the tree branch scraping the window; I look for shadows on the hallway walls.

THE MOTHERLAND IS BLEEDING

I

There are communists in the funhouse is a common Danish phrase for being on one's period.

The curse, on the rag, Aunt Flo, riding the cotton pony, crimson tide, red badge of courage, time of the month, lady business. Just a few of the euphemisms Americans have for menstruation.

In Turkey, a girl having her period might whisper to a friend, *the Motherland is bleeding.*

From the onset of her period through menopause, a woman will have approximately four-hundred-and-fifty periods.

Based on the number above, the average woman will spend around seven years of her life on her period.

In Japan, having a girl's day signals, to those who must know, that a woman or girl is menstruating.

The average American woman spends about thirteen dollars a month on menstrual products, which amounts to approximately $6,300 over the course of a woman's reproductive lifetime. Colloquially knows as *The Pink Tax.*

Thirty of the fifty states in America tax period products because they are considered "non-essential goods."

Recent studies show that two out of three low-income women in the U.S. have difficulty paying for basic period products.

In Finland, a young man might ask his girlfriend if she has mad cow disease when she declines sex during her period.

2

Lily starts her period during gym, the fall of eighth grade. In the locker room, when she pulls down her shorts in the bathroom stall, there it is: a brownish stain against her white cotton underwear. She expects red, not brown, but her mother has told her nothing of periods. The information Lily has gathered from other girls covers only tampons and cramps.

All day she feels a throbbing ache low across her belly. I begat my period, she thinks to herself. *Begat.* She's pretty sure she's using the word wrong, but it sounds appropriately serious, sophisticated. Crowded into a locker room stall, her friend Elizabeth, shows her how to insert a tampon. At home, Lily pushes her stained underwear to the back of the top shelf of her closet. She cannot bring herself to tell her mother she has begat her period.

When Elizabeth got her period, her mother bought her a gift, but this strikes Lily as a white person thing to do, and she wouldn't expect such a gesture from her own. Her Vietnamese mother doesn't understand such rituals in the same way she doesn't understand sleepovers or taking your daughter shopping for her first bra. It's Lily's older sister who gives Lily two hand-me-down bras when Elyse outgrows them.

Each time she gets her period, Lily contemplates telling her mother, but she cannot bring herself to do so. Soon there is a pile of stained underwear on the top shelf of her closet. Lily's parents do the laundry, and it occurs to her that she could start doing it herself. Her mother never asks Lily if she's gotten her period though she must notice the tampons and pads in the linen closet are disappearing more quickly than they used to. Lily waits and waits until one day her mother yells to her to come upstairs immediately, and Lily burns with shame.

IIII

Beget: to give rise to or bring about. Alternatively: to bring a child into existence by the process of reproduction. Begat: past tense of beget.

In middle school, Elizabeth tells Lily that she cannot get pregnant while on her period. Lily, the smarter of the two, tells Elizabeth she's wrong. Neither has sex until college.

Lily gives birth to her first child at thirty-four. She is told that pregnancies after thirty-five are called geriatric pregnancies. She has apparently gotten in just under the wire.

While pregnant, Lily does not glow. Late at night, she feels like she can't breathe, and she is convinced she might swallow her tongue.

Lily's sister Elyse cannot get pregnant. She is even more geriatric than Lily and has a tilted uterus to boot.

When Lily's mother is fifty-four, she has a total hysterectomy, which makes her seem crazy for an entire year.

When Lily's husband gets a vasectomy and she goes off the pill, her periods are so heavy she takes to sleeping on her son's recently discarded Lightning McQueen blanket.

A friend tells Lily about endometrial ablation, a procedure women have so they don't bleed so heavily. This involves surgically destroying the uterine lining to reduce blood flow.

Lily is not interested in surgically destroying any part of her body and so she continues to spread her Lightening McQueen blanket across the bedsheets each month when the communists are in the funhouse.

HUSKED

My teeth start falling out three weeks after my father dies. Yes, just like that. I'm eating cereal while watching *Home Alone* for at least the tenth time with my daughter, and I feel a pinch near my back left molar then something sharp under my tongue. In the palm of my hand the tooth doesn't even look like a tooth. The crown of it does, but instead of tapering down into a few healthy roots, there is a single sad-looking root, and when I turn the tooth over in my palm, it is empty, eaten away inside like a husk. My daughter peers over and considers the tooth. "Put it under your pillow, Mama." And then right back to her movie, like it's normal for an adult to lose a tooth while eating cereal. In her defense, she is only three.

I lose one more before I get in to see the dentist, who immediately refers me to a specialist. I've collected my teeth in a small container that used to hold foam earplugs, and when he puts them on a slide under a bright light, I'm embarrassed by how diseased they look—like rotten kernels of corn. He reaches into my mouth and gently pushes each of my teeth, testing to see which ones wiggle, he explains. He's so close I smell his breath through his hygienic mask; it smells like cinnamon, which makes me think of the pancakes with cinnamon my daughter demands every morning. My stomach growls, and I swear it's the first whine of hunger I've felt since my father had a massive stroke two months ago.

I think of the hospital, all those machines and tubes, all those decisions no one wanted to make, which we eventually did make, my mother finally agreeing with my siblings and me that it was time to "pull the fucking plug." My father's words, every time he joked about dying, which he did a lot once he hit seventy. "You know what to do," he'd say. "Pull that fucking plug if you have to." He also made it known, on more than one occasion, that his preference for a funeral would be for us to put him on a wooden raft, set it on fire, and push it out into the bay, Viking style. But for all his jokes about death, he left all decisions up to my mother, who could not do what needed to be done until my father had wasted away to almost nothing and was completely unresponsive.

My father, who taught us to bodysurf in pounding waves, who held us on skis between his skis and hurled us down hills, who ate and drank like an actual Viking, who played in a basketball league until he was seventy, who shuffle-jogged up until he was eighty, is dead. "Eighty is the new sixty-five," I'd told him the last time I'd shuffle-jogged with him. He'd look at me mid-shuffle and raised his shaggy brows. "Get real. Eighty is eighty," he said and kept on shuffling.

When the specialist shows me the X-rays of my bottom front teeth, which are the front-runners for surgical extraction, I think their roots look like tiny hourglasses, nipped in at the middle with just a very small flare of white on either side. External root resorption, the specialist says while tapping a finger against the film he's tacked up on a light box. "See how it looks like there's something eating at the roots? Well, that's because there is." And then he rattles off the details, most of which I have trouble following. He uses words like *cementin, granulomatous, fibro-osseous tissue.* Words that mean nothing to me. And some that do—*insidious, invasive, inflammatory.* The something eating away at my roots? It's me. Attacking myself—a type of autoimmune response. When I ask why my immune system would signal this attack, he offers a host of reasons: trauma, overzealous orthodontic movement, bleaching, chemotherapy. The list goes on, but all I hear is *trauma.*

"It all makes sense," I interrupt, "my father died three weeks ago. And then my teeth started falling out." The doctor gives me a look like the one I give my daughter when she says the alphabet and skips over *g, h,* and *i* entirely. "I meant oral trauma. Like tooth grinding or an injury to the mouth. And just for the record, you're definitely a grinder." I want to ask him how he knows, for sure, that it's the grinding trauma and not my father's death trauma that's making my teeth fall out. Prove it, I want to demand.

In the weeks my father lay in the hospital, his body shrank with alarming speed, as if death came each night for its pound of flesh until, finally, we let death take my father entirely. We spent weeks talking to my unresponsive father, holding his hand and patting it lightly, careful to avoid the tubing and wires sprouting from various parts of him. We moistened his lips with a tiny sponge on a stick and joked about dipping it in Jameson instead of water.

When I held my father's hand, it was cold and dry. When I held my father's hand, I remembered his body in motion—the powerful freestyle strokes that propelled him across water, white-knuckled pull-ups from the chin-up bar in his garage, his arms wrapped around my daughter in the "bone-crusher" hugs she begged him for. I want to believe that he is here with me still, that memory keeps him close, but this is a weak balm. Easily wiped away. I understand now that when I held my father's hand in the hospital, I held hands with death, for my father had fled all those weeks before and left only his body, just the loose husk of who he once was.

PARTY STORIES

I saved someone's life once. A woman drowning in a river, and good thing, because it's my go-to party story. People love a story where someone almost dies. Really, that's the part they love—that someone almost died. Not that a hero stepped in to save the day. People are morbid fucks when it comes right down to it. But I was that hero. Me.

And I'm skinny as a rail, not an inch of muscle on me, so people get even more excited when I tell them I saved a drowner; they take a look at my scrawny ass and think, *If she can save someone, I definitely can. Hell, I can probably save more than one person.* If it's a man I'm talking to, he adds in my being a woman and probably thinks he could save a boatload of people from drowning.

But me, I just saved the one. Briana, a cousin of Tonya's, who came down to the river to swim with a group of us who work at Motley Kitchen. In the summer, when our shift is over, we like to swim at the Holy Hole, which is what we call our part of the river. It's always dark and cool by the water, and the moon is fat, like Tonya. And beautiful, also like Tonya. She's always telling me she'd kill to be skinny like me, but I think Tonya is perfect. It's her ex-husband who made her feel ugly. Pete, who used to call her a cow and who I'm pretty sure socked her around some. She wouldn't ever admit it, but you can only come to work with so many black eyes and klutz stories before people catch on. Pete's the kind of guy whose party story involves group sex, and he tells it with pride. That's Pete. Tonya left him two years ago, but it took her years to work up to it, putting up with his bullshit and God knows what else, but she did it because Tonya's strong. She's strong in a quiet way, which is why most people don't see this about her. Except me. I know she's strong.

So anyway, we like to swim in the river after work. We're sweaty, we smell like smoke and grease, and we're tired as anything, but nothing feels better than dunking under that cold water, feeling the current rush against our throbbing legs, wiping clean a night of customers, some rude, others so nice and friendly it hurts. Tonya treats every customer with kindness, even the rude or obnoxious ones. Once, when I told a pushy trucker who wanted my number that it was 1-800-Never-Gonna-Happen, she told me she wished she could put a customer in his place like that. Brave, she even called it! I wanted to tell her that talking brave isn't the same thing as being brave, but I just shrugged my shoulders and helped her bus her tables. When she's working, Tonya hums to herself softly. Listening to the smooth, low rhythm of her voice reminds me of being in the water—effortless and cool.

So, Briana, the cousin, is visiting from Indiana, and Tonya's got to work, which means Briana hangs out at the bar, waiting for Tonya's shift to end, taking advantage of the free drinks she's getting 'cause Duane, the bartender, thinks she's cute. Briana's not fat and beautiful like Tonya. No, Briana's got muscles everywhere—almost like a man. Her biceps pop when she raises her beer for a swig, and her legs look strong enough to crush someone between them. I wonder what it might feel like to have muscles like that, for people to see how strong you are just by looking at you.

We finally get off work and head to the river—me, Tonya, Briana, Duane, and Mickey, one of the dishwashers. Mickey has a joint, and we sit on the big rock where the current picks up to smoke. The boulder feels smooth and cool, and I lean back and admire the moon. I can feel Tonya next to me, even if we're not touching. I peer out the corner of my eye and see those gorgeous, thick thighs of hers, and I want to touch them. But I just run my hands over the cool rock beneath me, stare back up at the swollen moon above me.

Duane howls like a wolf and cannonballs off the boulder into the cold rushing water below. The thing about this part of the river is that it gets about twelve feet deep in the bend of water we swim in, then it gets real shallow, real quick, on either side of the Holy Hole. *Come on in, Tonya's cousin!* Duane yells over to Briana, and I don't want to watch this mating ritual go down, so I slide to the edge of the boulder and push off into the water below.

I like to let myself sink until I can feel the silky cold mud and smooth stones at the bottom of the river. I squish my toes through the mud. Everything is muted and cool and dark, and I can't feel where my body ends and the water begins. It is my favorite feeling in this world. When I can't hold my breath any longer, I shoot myself up to the surface of the river to fill my lungs.

Briana is just starting to tiptoe into the river from the bank instead of dropping in off the boulder like the rest of us. It's strange to see such a muscular creature move so tentatively through the shallows; I'd assumed she would have used those legs of hers to spring herself off the boulder into some kind of fancy flip or dive. Why have all those muscles if you're not gonna use them? But who am I to judge? Briana is hugging herself with her huge biceps and whimpering about how cold it is. I'm treading water against the current in the Holy Hole 'cause it's good exercise and the only exercise I do. Briana does her baby steps closer to the hole, and I call out to her, "Watch it. It gets deep real fast and the current picks up." *Idiot* is what I'm thinking. Get in or get out, but stop making a show of it.

And then Briana slips under. One minute she's standing and holding herself with her big ole guns, and the next, just the surface of the water, moving like the only thing in it is the current. It is almost graceful, really, except for what comes next, which is that Briana's head breaks the surface, hair pasted across her forehead and over her eyes, gulping and gasping and yelling for help before letting the water swallow her back up.

I pause for just a few seconds, thinking she's playing, that no one who can't swim would be dumb enough to get into a river past their ankles. In those few seconds I notice Duane reclined over in the shallows by the bank, and I hear Micky yelling, *What the fuck is she doing?* Then Tonya's clear voice rings through the night, "She can barely swim!" And that's when I dive down for Briana.

Underneath the water it's dark, and silt and mud mix about and make it even harder to see, but it's not like it matters much because there's no way to miss the thrashing just a few feet away from me. Briana is down close to the bottom, and as I'm swimming toward her, she pushes off the muddy riverbed, flapping wildly upward, so I surface with her, let her grab on to my arm. Now I know that isn't what you're supposed to do, but it's all I know in that moment, so I do it.

But does Briana grab my arm like she's clearly supposed to? No! She grabs the tops of my shoulders, hair still plastered over her eyes, somehow with the breath to sob and yell, *Help me*, and she clamps her hands down on my shoulders, pushing me under, using me like some kind of human raft she's trying to get on top of. And that's not the worst part: she's thrashing hard, and those kicks have to land somewhere, that somewhere being my gut, and then I'm fully submerged, and now she's sinking us both down toward that muddy bottom, and I swear to God it feels like she must weigh three hundred pounds, and all I can think is that this bag of muscles is gonna drown me. She's gonna kill me. I'm gonna drown trying to save someone from drowning.

I don't think something ever struck me as clear as the fact that she was going to drown us both, and that's when I start trying to get her off of me—punching, as best as I could underwater, at her rock hard abs, her chest, I may have even gone for her head—all the while twisting and pushing away from her until I finally break free and swim to the surface. I'm gasping for air, hoping she has the sense to push off the bottom again 'cause there's no way

I'm diving back down for her. And there she is, just seconds after me, sputtering, reaching for me, and this time I yell, "Grab my arm!" and I push back from her so she can't reach any other part of me, just my forearm. I use my free arm to paddle, and I kick hard toward the shallows where Duane is coming toward us.

Briana sits in a heap on the bank, sobbing, and Tonya hugs her, shushing her like a baby. I wait for Tonya to check on me, but it's Duane and Mickey who huddle around me telling me I'm a hero. They say they were about to dive down, but it looked like I could handle it. Why in God's hell would you think that, I want to ask, but I stay quiet 'cause who doesn't want to be called a hero? I watch Tonya hug Briana until Briana gets up and walks over to me—all unsteady and snotty like some kind of monstrous toddler. I know it's mean to describe her like this 'cause she was scared down there, but I was too, and you don't see me blubbering all over everyone.

"You saved my life," Briana tells me, like I don't already know it. "You saved my life," she keeps repeating. And I pat her on the shoulder and say it's okay just to get her to shut up. Tonya comes over and says it's time to go home.

She turns to me and looks at me with those brown eyes, little flecks of gold shot through, and says, "Thank God you were here, Holly. Thank God." She jerks her head at Duane and Mickey. "These two are worthless, and you know how slow I am. You saved her, Holly."

I want Tonya to keep going, but she trudges up the bank behind Briana to leave. Mickey and Duane drive me home, keep calling me a hero. I tell them how Briana felt as heavy as an iron anchor, how tight her grip was, how I punched and pushed at her underwater to free myself. I tell them she was going to drown me, and I even tell them that I wanted to save myself more than anything.

What I don't tell them, what I don't tell anyone when I tell my best party story, is that I needed to survive because I had to hear Tonya's voice again—the silvery sound of it when she hums at work. I tell myself that I leave this part out because I know what makes a good party story. People want to hear about slipping beneath the surface, about punching and thrashing: they want to feel death come close. They want to break the surface and be called a hero, so I give them what they want.

$X + Y$ = SOMETHING

We know about Mr. Donnelly, who leans in close when he teaches us algebra, the rattle of a spearmint LifeSavers clicking against his teeth, minty breath that makes the skin on the backs of our necks prickle and cool.

Mr. Donnelly, who, rumor has it, once told another class that he was attracted to "women like Jules," who is a sophomore but looks twenty-seven. Jules denies that ever happened. But we know about Jules too.

Mr. Donnelly, who rolls up his shirtsleeves so we can see the muscles in his forearms ripple when he grips the chalk. Thick brown hair covers his arms like the ivy that crawls up the walls of our school's courtyard.

His pants are too tight, and it's impossible not to stare at his crotch when he sits on his desk, his legs splayed man style. We wonder if he does this on purpose. Some of us try to avert our eyes, but most of us stare because it's like he's daring us to, and we're not afraid of Mr. Donnelly.

We know about Mr. Donnelly, who talks too much about college at Harvard while teaching fifteen-year-old girls that X + Y = something. He tells us that algebra is beautiful. That Mr. Donnelly equates algebra with beauty makes it that much clearer he can't be trusted.

Mr. Donnelly, who touches us on our wrists when he kneels down beside our desks to help with an equation. Mr. Donnelly, who we once saw at a restaurant with a woman who looked like Jules. Some of us spread the rumor that it was definitely Jules. No doubt about it.

Jules with her long black curls, the eyeliner that sweeps out from her eyelids like she's some kind of teenage Cleopatra. A queen lording her perfect breasts over us—cleavage that always manages to peek out no matter that we all wear white oxfords beneath navy V-necked sweaters. It takes a real commitment to showcase anything in our school uniforms. We know. We've tried.

"The beauty of algebra," Mr. Donnelly tells us, "is that we use it to understand real-world phenomena all the time. Gravity, salary increases over time, the population growth of rabbits!" When he gives that last example about rabbits, he stares right at Jules, and we know it's because he's thinking about rabbit-fucking her.

We know what happens after school when Jules goes to Mr. Donnelly's office to get help with algebra, which she's acing, and when we corner her in the locker room to try and make her tell us just what the fuck is up with her and Mr. Donnelly, Jules gets a faraway look in her eyes like she's moved on to some other place and isn't standing with the rest of us on the slick tiled floor of a room that reeks of chlorine, sweat, and wanting. We watch what looks like the tremor of her plump, glossy lips—the start of a smile or maybe the start of something else entirely.

YOUR CHILD'S PROGRESS

I sit in a child's plastic chair across from Freida's teacher in room full of cozy book corners, small worktables, trays of wooden cubes and sand, boxes of costumes and puppets. Across the room, my little girl builds wobbly cardboard brick towers until they're taller than her, and then she knocks them down with the chop of her small but powerful leg, and her long, dark hair swings back and forth with the force of her kick. Freida is a smart, kind, and funny child. I'm not a mother who thinks her child is perfect—Freida is also stubborn, loud, and rambunctious. There have been times where I've wanted to tape her mouth shut when she's yelling or talking nonstop for what seems like hours. I am prepared to hear both the good and the bad in my child's very first parent-teacher conference.

Mrs. Butterworth, her real name, is a small woman with white-blond hair and skin so pale I can see a vein pulsing near her delicate collarbone. With a name like Mrs. Butterworth, her petite stature, and pristine blond bob, she seems made for teaching preschool. Born for it, really. But when Mrs. Butterworth opens her mouth to conference about my daughter, her voice is deep and gravelly. Though I've heard her speak before, at orientation, it always seems odd to hear such a rough voice come out of a woman who seems, in every other way, to evoke nurturing lightness. Mrs. Butterworth sounds like a drill sergeant.

In front of me, Mrs. Butterworth has placed a three-page progress report to guide our conference discussion about Freida. I notice that each time Freida destroys a tower, her preschool teacher flinches. "To begin with, I just want to say that Freida is a wonderful little girl. So full of potential," Mrs. Butterworth rasps. "But we're encountering several issues with her behavior in the classroom." I shift in my miniature chair, trying to find a comfortable position to relieve the pressure in my knees, which are locked up from contorting my body into a child-sized seat. I resent Mrs. Butterworth for putting us in these chairs. I am easily a foot taller than her. "Issues?" I try to make my voice light. My face bright.

"She has trouble following directions, particularly when we transition from activity to activity. It's quite disruptive for the other children."

I glance at Freida across the room. She is placing brick upon brick and talking to herself. My child is energetic, yes. She can be loud, yes. She has trouble following directions, yes. She is also four. I remember having my desk dragged to the front of the room in kindergarten so my teacher could *keep an eye on me.* Mrs. Weiss—an older white woman with thin, papery lips and closely cropped gray hair, who smelled like bleach and who once, after I used the bathroom, asked if I'd had a BM. I had no idea what she was talking about, but it seemed so accusatory that I remember crying. I never felt anything but afraid and in trouble in that woman's classroom.

"Can you give me a more specific sense of how she's disruptive?" I ask Mrs. Butterworth and tilt my head in a way I think seems inquisitive and friendly. My knees throb.

"Of course! I've listed several examples here." Mrs. Butterworth smiles, and her top lip reveals a swath of her slick, pink gums. She taps one of the pages in front of her with a pencil tip. Freida's progress report has bulleted points shaped like the leaves of a flower. I count four flowers beneath the subtitle "Issues":

- Freida often refuses to transition from reading rug time to math work. The classroom assistant, Mr. Scott, often has to spend much of what should be Freida's math time getting her from the reading rug to her worktable.
- Freida has a habit of announcing that she is bored when we are on the learning circle, and I'm conducting a lesson. This riles up the other children who follow her lead and begin to repeat, "I'm bored, I'm bored, I bored . . ." We've lost out on several lessons because of this.
- Freida seems to lack an awareness of her body and voice in the classroom space. She tends to yell and run indoors even though we stress that running and yelling are outside behaviors.
- Freida has trouble sitting in her chair during work time and often gets up and interrupts other children in their workspaces.

Beneath "Issues" is a section subtitled "Strengths":

- Freida is kind and inclusive with her classmates.
- Freida seeks out the Love Light Patch every single day—she is a loving child.

It's hard not to notice the specificity of Freida's issues, while her strengths remain rather abstract and generic. My knee joints feel as if they're about to pop, so I lean back as much as I can in my miniature chair and stretch my legs, bumping the table in the process so that Mrs. Butterworth's papers are jostled and her pencil falls to the floor. I don't move to pick up the pencil for her. In the corner of the room, I hear Freida's small roar as she destroys another tower. But I just keep staring at Mrs. Butterworth, who, for the first time in our conference, looks uncomfortable in her Lilliputian chair.

"I'm sorry if Freida has been disruptive," I say, and Mrs. Butterworth seems to relax. "But nothing you've listed here seems especially out of the ordinary given Freida's age." Before I'm even finished, Mrs. Butterworth is shaking her head in disagreement, her lips a thin, flat line.

"Oh no," she tells me. "All of the children in this group have adjusted to classroom expectations by this point in the school year." She waits for me to respond, but why bother when I can tell Mrs. Butterworth has already decided what kind of child Freida is. There is a peremptory air to her pronouncement about the other children that makes it clear to me she can only see Freida as a bad kind of exceptional.

I've spent much of my life contorting my long body into small spaces, making my face bright when it is not naturally so, my voice light when I feel dark. My daughter, with her loud, demanding voice and perpetual-motion body, will always be too much for a Mrs. Butterworth. I sent her to this school with its trays full of wooden math cubes, its Love Light Patch celebrating warmth and happiness, its little dishwashing station, its "method of hands-on learning and collaborative play," so that my girl would start school differently than I had. Tears and more tears in a room that reeked of bleach and where I spent most of my time sitting next to Mrs. Weiss at the front of the room while other children played. *Trouble,* I remember her whispering at me. *You're trouble.* My mother was a good mother, but in her culture, one didn't question a teacher's practices, one adapted. More than once, I ran the two blocks home after asking to go to the bathroom, and each time my mother gently dragged me back to school, my baby sister strapped to the front of her chest.

I reach my arms over my head and stretch myself out fully, then lean forward quickly and snatch Mrs. Butterworth's progress report on Freida. I crumple the papers into satisfying little balls in my fists and drop them on the table. A gravelly-throated *stop* erupts from Mrs. Butterworth. She scoots back her chair to stand, and I relish the fact that she has to look up at me. I dread the task of finding my daughter another school, but for now I simply collect her, hard at work on another tower of bricks. Freida takes my hand and glances up at me with her shiny dark eyes. "On the count of three," I tell her, and we each snap out a leg and send those bricks flying.

THEY SAY THE LIGHT IS MAGICAL

They say Paris is the most beautiful city on earth. The most romantic. That springtime in Paris is a revelation. They say the light in Paris is magical. They go on about the cheese, the wine, the pastries. But maybe Paris is also dog crap everywhere and the smell of urine coating the metro. Paris is also the banlieues, the no-go zones, the brutalist towers that ring the outskirts of what they say is the most beautiful city on earth. City of love. City of light.

Maybe Paris is the place all your mother's people were relocated after a war in a country colonized by the French. Perhaps the city is your grandparents' one-room apartment, just beyond the magical light of Paris proper, where, as a child, you realize they get food from the government because they're poor, because everything they had was lost to the war. Maybe Paris is the understanding that a doctor in a tiny southeast Asian country doesn't translate to a doctor in the most beautiful city on earth. Even if your grandfather speaks and writes the language of his colonizer fluently. Even if he's brilliant. Even if he's done everything that has been asked of him.

Maybe, for some, Paris is nothing like they say. Not magical or beautiful, but yes, maybe, sometimes a revelation. Like the time you're eleven and walking the streets of Paris with your mother, and a man smiles at you and points down, at his penis, which is flopping out of his unzipped pants. You've never seen a grown man's penis in real life and are stunned—yes, stunned—by how strange it is. Thomas Jefferson is said to have proclaimed that "a walk about Paris will provide lessons in history, beauty, and in the point of life." Maybe there was a lesson in that man wagging his penis at you that you still haven't figured out.

For you, Paris is a pidgin of Vietnamese, Cambodian, and French darting through the air; it is bánh xèo, gỏi cuốn, chả giò, phở, and White Rabbit candies. For you, Paris is helping your pépé with his English—his quick smile, his curiosity, his massive appetite for learning even after all that's he's lost. Paris is walking to the corner market to buy Pépé a lemon sorbet that comes in a small frozen lemon half—a treat in which he finds genuine delight.

For you, Paris is the shrine to your dead uncles—oranges, incense, photographs, a small statue of Buddha—that your mémé tends to. Paris is the sadness that never leaves her face, the anxious tapping of her fists against her thighs as she stands in her narrow kitchen. Paris is Mémé, Pépé, their ten remaining children, their seventeen grandchildren, and the ghosts of the dead.

RINGED

She bought it in a fit of joy, soon after he proposed. A string of steel rings of varying sizes that could be hung from the ceiling. A modernist mobile. A ring for her and a ring, technically rings, for him. Why should she be the only one ringed for the engagement? The circles hung in the living room and glinted in the afternoon sunlight that streamed through their windows.

A year later, the rings clank lightly when a gust of air swings in with the front door. An alarm that lets her know when he arrives home. Friends comment on the mobile, and she enjoys telling the story of why she bought it. Those glimmering rings still make her feel powerful, as does her decision to keep her last name, which makes her feel smarter than women who take their husband's; she hasn't yet realized how juvenile such sentiments are. She and her friends like to talk about the institution of marriage, how they did it for the tax breaks, how hard it is to raise a kid without it, particularly in their state, somewhere in the middle, where people marry young and never have just one child.

She doesn't have one yet. A child, that is. But she knows she will. Just like she knew, for all her rants against marriage, that one day she'd marry. What she doesn't know yet is how much she'll love that baby once it comes. How much she'll obsess over those tiny hands, her satiny skin, the bracelets of fat creases that ring her wrists. She doesn't yet know that when the baby sighs and gurgles in her sleep, she and her husband will press their faces into their pillows and laugh, so fearful of waking the child swaddled tight in the middle of the bed between them.

She also doesn't know yet that no matter how much she and her husband love their baby, it won't be enough to hold them all together. That by the time the little girl is three, they'll be separated. Divorced just before the child's fourth birthday. She doesn't know that the last time the front door slams and those rings clatter against each other, it will be the last time. The woman does not know the restlessness she will feel at home with her young child, no matter how much she loves her. She does not know how reckless she will become with her husband, her marriage, her child. She does not know, yet, that some things cannot be forgiven. She doesn't know the guilt she'll feel for many years after her marriage ends—less sharp as the years pass but still there, hovering, like a ghost in the background.

The woman doesn't know that it will mostly be her and her daughter, on their own, like the marriage never happened, like the rings were never exchanged. She doesn't yet know that her ex will remarry, that her daughter will have two half-siblings who look so much like her child it seems possible she gave birth to these children with whom she shares no blood relation. All she knows when she buys that string of steel rings for her soon-to-be husband is that her love is so large one ring is not enough.

WE WONDER

We wonder about the man across the street for a long time. The way he hacks at his bushes with an axe without rhyme or reason, without any sort of plan. When he finishes, the shrubs look like Jack's scalp after we held him down and buzzed his hair—patchy and angry. Raw and hurting.

We wonder about the man's cycling outfit, which he puts on every day at five o'clock sharp. Not shorts and a jersey, like a normal person, but a tight one-piece. A spandex athletic romper. There he goes in his romper, we say, as he pedals furiously down our street. We comment on his crotch, how it bulges out in a way that we can only call disgusting.

We are walking down the street, and the man comes by and offers us each a rose from the bouquet he holds. It is near to Valentine's Day, and none of us has ever been offered a rose. Candy hearts that say *Be Mine* or *You're Sweet* are the most we've been given and only because we are all made to give each other such things at school. Cheap flimsy cards that read *You're out of this world* with a spaceship blasting off, to which we add balls. We take the man's roses and run. We wonder why a grown man would do such thing.

We are growing. Child-women. In some cultures, girls our age are married. But in our world, we pedal our bikes to the beach or to get ice cream that melts as we ride one-handed and cocksure. We ride in packs and wear our bikinis and nothing else. Or tiny shorts and sports bras. We wear our helmets until we are out of sight and then stuff them in our backpacks. We are whippet thin or carry a layer or two of pudge. We chatter, chatter, chatter as we ride. We stare at our reflections every time we pass a window.

We wonder why the man across the street doesn't have a wife or a girlfriend. A husband or a boyfriend. We don't know grown men who don't come in a pair, and we are suspicious. One of us pays three dollars to check the sex offender registry for our neighborhood. We are sure he has offended. Why else would he be alone at his age? We know about pedophiles, have been warned forever of this sort of danger. He's not on any registry, but that doesn't mean he isn't a pervert, we say. Our ponytails swing violently as we nod in agreement.

It is up to us to save the unsuspecting. The most daring of us writes a note: *We know what you are*, it says in fat, curly letters that crowd up against each other. The fastest runner among us darts across the street and slips the note in his mailbox. We watch and wait for what seems like forever. We grow impatient and ride our bikes to the pool, push boys we know into the water, get kicked out. We go back on watch and make the weakest in our group go check his mailbox. The note is gone. We wonder if he's afraid. We wonder what he will do when he finds out it was us. We creep among the bushes and watch and wait until we can't wait anymore, and then we run out on to the lawn and twirl in circles until we are so dizzy we can barely see what's in front of us.

HEAT

The summer Lily turned fourteen, people were dropping like flies. A heat wave steamrolled across the Midwest, and it hadn't dipped below ninety-five degrees in Chicago the whole month of July. People lumbered about in heat stupors, and the news put out warnings against being outside too long and not drinking enough water. Old men and women were found dead in their apartments, smothered, blotted out by the heat. As of July 21, forty-one people had died. It didn't get cooler in the early dawn or at night. This was a thick, unwavering heat, something you could reach out and touch, open your mouth and take a bite out of any time of the day or night—not a dry heat that got sucked up into the darkness and offered some relief. The city set up emergency cooling centers: fluorescent-lit church basements, community centers with folding chairs, coolers of water, and blasts of icy cold air.

Lily saw the cooling centers on the news. She lived in a town north of the city—a "village" was what they called it on the sign that welcomed you. A village built along Lake Michigan: Big old houses, parks every other block, schools people moved there for. Lily's parents claimed it was a fluke, pure luck that they ended up there. They'd fled from their first house in a town not far away. Her mother loved to repeat the various racial injustices she'd suffered at the hands of their old neighbors. Recalling the stories seemed to energize her mother and, strangely, Lily always thought, to bring her mom a certain amount of joy.

Lily's mother was Vietnamese, and her father white, and they were never sure what bothered the neighbors (a family of Greek Americans) most: that he was American, that she was Vietnamese, that they'd married, that they weren't Greek. All this Lily heard secondhand; she was only a baby when they moved to the house they now lived in. But she'd grown up hearing stories of the neighbors' young daughter calling her sister Elyse a "dirty chink" and then spitting on her, or the time the neighbor called her mother a "lazy Filipina" because Lily's mom didn't know it was customary to shovel the front walk when it snowed. "She couldn't even tell what kind of Asian I am!," her mother always exclaimed.

If Lily and her family happened to drive anywhere in the vicinity of the old house now, her mother would grimace and shake her head. Sometimes she would look at Lily and say, "Never marry a Greek." Other times she would smile. "Thank God for the Greeks," she would say to no one in particular. Lily's mother credited the neighbors as the reason she and Lily's father ended up where they did.

It was in this "village"—where no one slammed window shades or spit on your kids, where people looked down on racial ignorance or kept their own prejudices stashed away at the back of the hall closet among the dusty galoshes and umbrellas—that Lily watched news reports of the elderly dying in their baking apartments in the city. She wrapped herself in a blanket, icy air piping in from discreet vents in the floors and ceilings, and watched interviews with the dead people's neighbors. They spoke of horrible smells and shook their heads sadly.

No one in Lily's town had died from the heat wave—not directly anyway—but the town was experiencing its own rash of freakish deaths. A man was found hanged by his neck (completely naked—that was the detail that stuck out most in Lily's head) from a tree in one of the parks. A woman was run over in front of the high school. And just one week after that, a man was dragged under the train and crushed when the shoulder bag holding his laptop was caught between the train car's sliding doors. Finally, just two days earlier, on July 19, Lily's grandpa, claw handed and slack faced from two strokes, had clenched her father's hand and softly growled his way out of the world. This last death (the only natural one and yet the most horrendous, in Lily's opinion) had left her inconsolable, and her father, in an attempt to soothe her, had told her over and over how her grandpa had clamped his hand so hard he thought it would break. "He was telling me he wanted to go," he said, trying to convince her. Lily would grab her father's hand and try to make him squeeze her hand in just the same way.

* * *

The day of her grandpa's funeral, Lily carried his coffin with her brother and four cousins out of St. Pat's in the city. In the church, she squeezed her hands together and chewed on her lip. She couldn't cry in front of people in the same way some people can't sneeze if they get to thinking about it. She got the urge; she could feel the strain in her throat and the beating of her pulse below her ears all during the funeral, especially when she grasped the bar of her grandpa's coffin, but that was all that would happen. In the car on the way to the cemetery, smooshed between a cousin and an aunt, she searched out the window for the emergency cooling centers she'd seen on TV. She thought maybe there would be big signs with lights signaling where to go for relief. But there was nothing of the sort.

They got home late, after a long dinner with cousins, aunts, and uncles. Lily went to her room, put on her running clothes, and went downstairs. Outside the house, the heat swallowed her up in waves. She started running immediately before she could register how humid and suffocating it was. She did this almost every night, ran for miles down the road along the lake until her T-shirt and shorts were soaked through, slick across her back and thighs, and she thought she'd die of thirst. Sometimes she waited until as late as nine-thirty to go, and her mother would yell that only crazy people ran that late at night and things about men hiding in bushes. Lily would slip past her, reassure her that she could run down Chestnut Road naked and nothing would happen to her. That was the kind of town they lived in. She might get a citation for indecent exposure from one of the policemen who cruised the streets aimlessly in shiny, white, sharklike patrol cars, but bodily harm was unlikely. That night, exhausted from the funeral, Lily's mother just told her not to run too far. "It's too hot" was all she said.

Lily ran until she reached Garrison Park, the place where the man had hanged himself at the end of June when the heat wave first hit Chicago. She always ran this route, but ever since that man had been found hanging from the tree at the entrance to the park, Lily made herself run to the tree and touch it before she turned to run home. But it wasn't the man she thought of; instead, it was the photo of the dead girl she'd glimpsed earlier that summer at her father's courthouse, hair tangled and mud splattered on her bare body: slick, bluish-white skin, limbs splayed out, eyes wide open. Eyes open to see the last seconds of someone stealing her life away. The girl wasn't from Lily's town, but the photo was more real than anything she'd heard about on TV. She'd felt sick when she'd seen the picture, strange and light, as if she'd fall over if she breathed in too deep.

Some people took their lives; some people's lives were taken from them. Either way, there was a moment in most cases where these people knew they were going to go. What about the girl in the photo? What was she thinking? What had Lily's grandpa been thinking? Lily's chest burned, and her throat ached slightly. That night, Lily slept with one arm outside the covers, her hand hanging off the mattress in the frigid air-conditioning of her room. She wasn't sure she believed she'd ever see her grandfather again, but she liked to think that if he did drift in while she was sleeping, he would squeeze her hand and wake her. Her friend Ted, whose mother died from cancer when they were in middle school, once told her that his mother had appeared to him soon after she'd died. He'd been walking home from school, and he'd seen her standing on someone's lawn. He claimed his mother's spirit waved to him once and then she was gone. If it could happen to Ted, why not her?

* * *

In the mornings, before she went to work at the beach by her house, Lily watched the news for the weather reports. She worked as a junior lifeguard at Alton Beach, one of the small beaches that dotted the east side of town. Her job basically consisted of looking to see if people had tokens when they came down to the beach. Lily sat at the kitchen counter, watching TV, and waited to see if anyone else had died from the heat wave. She wanted to count murders as heat wave deaths because she'd read somewhere that the murder rates went up in cities when it got extremely hot. On the morning news, no one had died from the heat, and Lily didn't watch to see if anyone had been murdered. She didn't actually keep tally of murders: It was just that lately if she saw one reported on the news, she believed that part of the reason it happened—small as it may have been—was the heat.

Lily's parents were on their hands and knees, pulling scraggly brown weeds from between the cracks in the patio. Her mother worked in a bathing suit and shorts, her shoulders and arms brown and glistening in the sun. Lily wondered if she would look like her mother when she was forty-five: skinny limbs but thickened through the middle with a belly that she claimed came from giving birth to Lily and her siblings. Every other house on the block had a crew of landscapers come in once a week to water, cut, and fertilize their yards into neat green squares and crisply trimmed hedges. The sound of summer in their neighborhood was the drone of lawn mowers and the clatter of hedge trimmers. There were always one or two wood-slatted trucks, the name of the landscaping company scrolled across the cab's doors, parked on the street. Sometimes the gardeners came down to the beach on their lunch break and ate in the shade of the trees in the park. Once in a while, in the afternoons when they'd finished their work, they'd come down and get out their wallets to buy a daily pass, so they could go down to the beach and swim for an hour. Lily always waved them through, telling them not to worry about the passes. The only people Lily charged were the high school kids or college students home on break, the ones who sauntered past her like she wasn't even sitting there. They usually had summer tokens dangling off the corner of their towels, but if they didn't, Lily made a show of pointing to the sign that listed the price for a daily pass even for residents.

Down at the beach, she dragged her chair and umbrella out of the office and up to her post. Before the lifeguards came on duty, she raked up the grime: weeds, sticks, and dead fish that washed up along the sand. Then she walked the two small stretches of beach that fanned out from either side of the pier, picking up wrappers or bottles that had appeared overnight. When she finished, she dove off the pier into water that was dark blue and freezing. The hotter it got that summer, the colder Lake Michigan felt. She undid the buoy line from the side of the pier, hooked it around her waist, and swam to the narrow iron divider that separated Alton Beach from a private beach that edged up against it. Once she had set the buoy line, she dove under the rope and swam out to the sandbar, where she usually waded around until she saw one of the lifeguards trekking down to the beach.

From the sandbar, she squinted back at the shore, at the massive houses that burst out from the bluff above the beach. Some had green lawns that sloped down to the beach's edge, and others had intricate staircases built down to the sand with deck landings every ten steps. They set out lounge chairs and umbrellas and tables, but Lily had never seen anyone actually come out and use them. She scanned the houses, the huge picture windows that faced the lake as she half floated, half walked backward toward the edge of the sandbar. She liked the unexpected drop, where her legs stepped back into nothing and she dipped under the water, past her shoulders and over her head. She came up for air and then dove back under and tried to follow the slope of sand down as far as she could. The sandbar shifted every few weeks. The edges were shaved down, dropped off, or the strip of sand grew wider and longer. Sometimes when she swam out to the sandbar, she had to swim around for a while before she could find it, the boundaries of where it began and ended washed away and relocated. She floated above the strip of sand, the sunlight two yellow pinpricks behind her closed eyes.

"Hey, Bones!" someone yelled. Lily quit floating and looked up to see Colin, the head lifeguard, standing with his hands on his hips at the end of the pier. "Are you getting paid to float around out there?" Lily usually spotted Colin, his tangled hair bleached almost to white by the sun, coming down the stairs to the beach. Most days, she'd be out of the water and on her way up to her token post before he could harass her. He stood on the beach waiting for her, his hands on his hips. He was always standing like that, arms flexed out, his shoulders hunched forward to make himself look bigger.

"You better be careful out there, Bones. You might just float away in the breeze one day."

Lily grabbed her towel, which he had slung over his shoulder, and walked over to the pier to dry off. Colin was older than her, seventeen, and the kind of guy who called all other guys by their last names. He wore beaded necklaces looped around his neck and skinny rope bracelets around his ankle. He was something of a soccer star at the high school, and he'd never called Lily anything but Bones since the first day she'd shown up for work. Lily had grown four inches in the past year, and her skin stretched tight across her frame like there wasn't enough of it. She was often embarrassed at the flatness of her body, but Colin was so clearly self-conscious of his own lanky frame that most of the time his comments slid over her. He talked about weights too much and stood with his hands on his hips because he thought it made him look bigger.

"You missed a spot." Colin grabbed her towel and tried to run it down the back of her thighs. Lily grabbed for her towel, but Colin jumped back out of her reach.

"Fine, keep it." Lily started walking up the stairs to her chair, wishing that she'd brought her T-shirt down with her. Something whipped across the back of her right calf, and she spun around to face Colin, who just stared at her and twirled her towel in a rat's tail. It made Lily cringe to think that at the beginning of the summer she'd tried to laugh along with Colin as if they were joking with each other: like friends who gave each other a hard time when she'd known it wasn't anything like that. "Fuck off, Colin."

"Oh, come on, Bones." He threw the towel at her hard, laughing. When he walked past her, he ran his finger across her shoulder and then licked his fingertip like he'd just dipped it into something. "Yummm. Caramel."

Upstairs, Lily sat under the umbrella and read. A few kids trickled down to the beach. Some old women, who always showed up with fly swatters and chairs, made their way past her. For the most part, the beach stayed pretty empty during the day. It was that kind of hot. People didn't even want to laze around in the water because it meant being outside. The beach was most crowded in the early evening when the heat of the day had let up a little and people felt like venturing out. Every so often Lily would sprint down the stairs to the water to cool off. Colin sat on the lifeguard chair, sunlight glaring off his sunglasses, serious, a whistle dangling from one hand. A few kids splashed around at the edge of the water. The other guard was stretched out in the shade, sleeping. They rotated on and off the chair. She didn't have to worry about Colin harassing her if there was anyone else around. He wouldn't say two words to her if another guard was nearby or people were on the beach. Lily dunked under and walked, drenched, up the stairs, back to her post.

Underneath one of the big maple trees in the park, there were some landscapers eating lunch. They had little coolers and brown paper bags, and Lily watched them trading things back and forth. Some of them lay back on the grass, others talked, the fast clip of their Spanish punctuated by laughter. Lily recognized some of the men who worked on the yards on her street. One of them waved at her, and she waved back.

* * *

Sitting at the kitchen counter, under one of the air-conditioning vents that sent bursts of cool air down the back of her T-shirt, Lily ate three ice cream sandwiches during her lunch break at home. Upstairs, she could hear the murmur of her parents and the opening and shutting of drawers and closets. The next day, her mother and her younger sister, Margot, would leave for France, where they spent a month each summer visiting her mother's family. Lily's mother was the only one who came as far west as the States, and she loved to go visit in the summer, where she could sit around with her sisters and talk a million miles a minute in a pidgin of Vietnamese, Cambodian, and French.

Lily's mother had postponed the trip indefinitely because of her grandpa's illness. Her mother's parents lived in a tiny ground-floor apartment in Paris, and when they went to visit, they all piled in to the apartment until their dad arrived at the end of the trip and they got to stay in a hotel for the final week. Lily's mother cooked every meal for her parents and hovered over them constantly. Lily and her siblings would spend most of their time playing cards with their pépé or going with their cousins to the public pool. At night, Lily rubbed her mémé's feet with Tiger Balm.

This was the first summer Lily would not make the trip to France with her mother and Margot. Her sister Elyse and brother, Max, had stopped going regularly when they'd started high school. For a few moments, she regretted the big show she'd made of not going because she had a summer job. She filled her water bottle and yelled up to her parents that she was going back to work. The only thing her mother called back to her was to "be careful." Not of the sun, not of anything in particular. Lily's mother was always telling her to be careful of something—a reflex like grabbing her arm when they crossed a street together.

Back at work, Lily took over for Joe, who was in charge of manning the token post while she was on break. As soon as he saw her coming across the park, he waved and hopped on his bike, shirtless and shoeless, a backpack slung across his shoulders. Lily didn't really know him but liked him because he only ever referred to Colin as *Asshole.* "Asshole wants you to tell people to keep their bikes in the park, not on the beach," or "Asshole's on fire with his new whistle," or, as he rode past, "Watch out, Asshole's in a mood today."

Not a single person came down all afternoon, and Lily finished reading her sixth book since she'd started the job. At five o'clock, she went down to the beach to sign out and pull in the buoy lines. There were two high school kids, a boy and a girl, sitting at the end of the pier, smoking and dangling their feet over the edge. An older woman and two little kids were at the far end of the beach, digging in the sand at the water's edge. Colin was taking down the umbrella from the guard chair and unhooking the little chalkboard that had the lake temperature scrawled on it.

* * *

Lily went into the office and took down the sign-in sheet from the wall. Colin came in behind her and threw the umbrella and chalkboard in the corner by the extra buoys and first-aid kits. She scribbled her name and filled in the "time out" box. She could feel Colin staring at her, and she didn't want to turn around. "Looks like you got burned, Bones." Colin pulled up on one strap of Lily's suit, away from her shoulder, exposing a strip of white skin, stark next to the dark brown of her shoulder. She twisted herself away from him, and the strap slapped against her shoulder when he let go. She tried to walk past him, and he blocked her, left and then right, laughing. Lily could see out the office door; she could hear the two little kids screaming for their grandma to come in the water.

"Don't you have better things to do?" She tried to walk past him again, but he grabbed her arms right above the elbows and pushed her slowly back toward the wall, laughing the whole time, like they were friends and this was fun. Outside the office, Lily heard people coming down the stairs to the beach. She could hear the rush of Spanish as the crew of landscapers walked past the office down the pier.

"You know," Colin said, letting go of her arms and stepping back a little. "You'd better stop letting those people in for free." Lily moved away from the wall, and

Colin pushed her back, his hands on her hips. Her shoulder blades slapped against the cold brick, and her head knocked against it slightly. Lily swung wildly at the side of his head, and he laughed, pinning her arms at her sides. His knees jabbed into her legs so she couldn't move.

"I know you let them in for free, Bones." Colin smiled, dug his fingers into her arms, and smashed his mouth against hers so hard that one of Lily's bottom teeth sliced the inside of her lip, and the rusty taste of blood filled her mouth. Strands of his bleached-out hair brushed across her eyelids and cheeks like dried, scratchy straw. She thought of the time she'd fallen off the banister and had the wind knocked out of her. She remembered the panic she'd felt when she tried to yell and cry for her mother and nothing came out, how she'd had to lie on the steps and wait for her breath to come back to her. She thought of her grandpa squeezing her father's hand. She opened her eyes, and she bit down hard—as hard as she could. Her teeth pierced through his bottom lip, soft and easy like through the pulp of an orange. He stumbled back, off her and on to the floor, his hands up against his chin, cupping his mouth. She watched the blood seep through his fingers.

She took the stairs up from the beach two at a time. She could hear the splash of water behind her, the sound of bodies breaking the surface of the water. Lily wiped the blood from her mouth as she ran, pressed her tongue against the cut on the inside of her lip. In the park, she stopped running, slowed down to catch her breath. She used the bottom of her T-shirt to wipe her face, sweeping back the hair plastered to her sweaty forehead and neck. She walked toward her house, pressing the T-shirt to her lips, and she remembered the girl in the photograph. In an elevator on the way up to see her father's new courtroom, Lily had stood behind two men discussing a case. One of them held a large black-and-white photo of the girl, naked with matted strands of hair covering her cheek and mouth. She was lying in a ditch, in a shallow puddle of water, mud streaked across her body, her neck twisted at an unnatural angle. Lily hadn't been able to tear her eyes away from the photo. She thought of her now, of the girl who was dead—not because of a heat wave or because she'd decided she'd had enough, not because she was old and it was time.

ONCE

In the attorney's painfully bland office, all beiges and sailboat paintings, I am sitting here, signing the papers that will finally dissolve us, papers that will end a year of rage and tantrums, like the time I plunged a knife into the hideous recliner chair that his father gave us as a wedding gift, gutting those cushions like my soon-to-be-ex used to gut a deer, or the time he dug up three evergreen trees in the middle of the night, yelling that I could take his house but not his evergreens, or the time I threw a vase at his head, and he laughed like a maniac when it shattered against the wall behind him—but what I think of as I sign the endless cascade of thick, expensive paper is how he once sliced up all the black olives from a jar and carefully placed them on the cheap delivery pizza that arrived without them, built a small set of stairs to our bed so our limpy dog, Cricket, could get in more easily, wrote and illustrated a story about Lulu and Bond (nicknames for our junk—completely disgusting, I know, but this was in the beginning when we were demented with lust), let my brother sleep on our couch for more than five months without complaint, got a perm just to make me laugh, carried me upstairs and downstairs when I broke my ankle instead of just letting me use my crutches like a normal person, wrote a song that made me sound better than I ever was, put up a tree swing in our backyard because I told him I'd always wanted one as a kid, made our bed every single day because he knew it was the household task I hated most, agreed that dogs were superior to children every time I said it even though he came from a family of seven and would have had kids in a heartbeat if I'd wanted them, gave me his undershirts to sleep in because I loved the smell of their soft worn-out cotton, held me when I cried every single day for months after my mother died, and had the decency to match every one of my petty tantrums during this year of divorce.

IN THE CORN FIELDS

It is nighttime in a college town, and a young woman weaves across the pedestrian mall, looking for the friends she lost at the last bar. College students stand on the street, shoving pizza down their throats, faces lit by the blue glow of their phones. Anika sits on a bench, pats her pocket for her phone, and finds that it, too, is lost.

Above her, the sky is full of stars because fields of corn and miles of gravel road surround the campus, and the little city's lights are no match for the sky above it. Most of the people that Anika knows at the university come from towns within the state. She grew up on a farm not far from the university, and she existed in a state of alarm for most of her first semester—so many cars, so much noise, so very many bars. But she's been at school for two years now and is comfortable enough to be a little tipsy and alone on a bench in the middle of town.

A woman, a student at the university like Anika, has recently gone missing while cycling the gravel roads beyond the town's borders. There are yellow ribbons tied everywhere, a symbol of hope that the missing woman might return or at least be found. A light to guide her home, explains the woman's parents when interviewed for the local newspaper. Earlier that week, the missing woman's bike is found in a wooded area twenty-five miles from town. It's been seventeen days since the woman disappeared, and media interest has waned, but with the discovery of her bike, a renewed energy surges through campus and town. Tattered ribbons are replaced with glossy new ones, fresh batches of flyers are delivered to all the shops and bars, and the missing woman climbs back up to the top of the news cycle.

Satiny ribbons are retied around the thick trunks of the oak trees that line campus, around signposts and stop-lights, wrapped carefully again around porch railings and mailbox posts. A shiny yellow ribbon is tied to the arm of the bench Anika sits on. She slides her fingers slowly over the smooth tails of the ribbon and then tugs gently on the silky fabric until it loosens enough to pull into a small, tidy pile of gold in her hands. She thinks of the fields of corn surrounding the farm where she grew up. Every summer of high school was spent detasseling corn with other teenagers and college kids. Anika remembers the summer the corn grew so high she could just barely reach the tassels—how easy it was to hide among those stalks, how good it felt to occasionally stretch out on the ground, stalks of corn rising up on either side of her. How hard and cool the dirt was beneath her body as she stretched her arms above her head—a few minutes of rest in a place no one could see her.

Anika rises from the bench to her feet. She tips back on her heels for a moment and then walks away from the center of the town toward her dorm. The yellow ribbon unravels from her fist as she walks, and when she turns the corner into the darkness beyond, it flutters from her hands to the ground where it will be trampled among the cigarette butts and greasy napkins by bar patrons who spill on to the sidewalks after last call.

NAMING THINGS

There is a fancy dinner at the college where Leila teaches and where she's seated between an older woman and the chair of the fine arts department. This is the kind of dinner that includes a mix of academics, board of trustees members, leaders from the community, and major donors. Student workers serve dinner. Leila hates these things but has made an exception because the person being honored is someone she admires.

The older woman on Leila's left introduces herself as Audrey. She peers at Leila's name tag and looks up at her face, back down at the name tag, up at her face, until she finally rattles out, "That's an interesting name. Leila. Where is it from?" Audrey's hair is in a puffy chignon, white with slightly blue undertones. Her knobby fingers are lined with shiny stone-sized rings, and she seems to enjoy the cloyingly sweet white wine being served. Leila launches into the story of her namesake—Leila, after her mother's childhood friend from France—Leila goes on and on because she knows that what this woman really wants to ask her is, "Where are you from?" which is, Leila understands, the polite way of asking, "What are you?"

After the story of Leila's name, Audrey takes a long sip of her bad wine before she says, "Hmmmmm. My husband taught history here for thirty years, and that name is from the Middle East. Not France." Leila isn't sure what Audrey's husband has to do with their conversation. Maybe his position makes the woman an authority on names? The woman's lips are dry and puckery, and the lipstick she's applied can't be absorbed by the tiny, desiccated tributaries that crisscross her lips. Leila feels a little bit sorry for her.

"Leila, Layla, Laila. You're right; it's a very popular name in the Middle East. But I'm named for my mother's childhood friend. From France." Leila smiles at Audrey, who stares at Leila with squinted eyes. Leila can tell she has annoyed Audrey and feels the juvenile pleasure of evading Audrey's unasked question.

After another sip of her chardonnay, the woman leans toward Leila conspiratorially and says, "Well, you're not one of them, are you?" She smiles widely and chases her comment with a loud, deep-throated laugh. Among the group of student-servers, there are two young women wearing hijabs, one of whom is busing empty salad plates on the other side of their table. Audrey is not looking at the server when she says this; she's looking right at Leila. Leila freezes and then looks at the server, who continues to bus plates and appears not to have heard the old woman.

Leila doesn't have a pithy reply because she's so surprised by Audrey's unabashed racism. She feels like an idiot as the warmth creeps up her neck and to her face. She feels the same way she did in college when she walked into a party and a guy called out to her, "Now here comes a Hawaiian girl," a big smile plastered across his face. When Leila told him, "I'm actually not Hawaiian," he'd simply retorted, "Then fuck you," and kept on walking. Leila had burned with embarrassment then as she did now. Which made no sense—what did she have to be embarrassed about? And why was it that twenty years later, Leila still couldn't respond to people like Audrey? Instead, Leila turns toward the man on her right, who is in deep conversation with the person on the other side of him. She stares stupidly at the podium, which is empty. She considers trying to shame Audrey but tells herself this would be like trying to shame a gargoyle. Absolutely pointless.

When the server in a hijab rounds the table and picks up Audrey's plate, the old woman grasps the young woman's forearm and smiles brightly up at her. "Thank you, sweetheart," Audrey rasps. "You're doing such a good job." The server beams back at the old woman, tells her, "Thanks." When the server picks up Leila's plate, their eyes meet and Leila smiles. The young woman doesn't return Leila's smile, nor does she frown, and, to Leila, the server's neutrality feels like a sharp slap that makes her face burn all the brighter.

WHEN GEORGIA SIMPSON AWAKES

When Georgia Simpson awakes, tangled in the blue sheets of an unfamiliar bed, she finds herself transformed into a giant slippery slug. She's been dreaming of her husband, a man with beautifully tanned skin and seemingly silver-blue eyes.

Beside the bulk of her wet, gelatinous new self lies a very large, furry brown rodent. His face, sharp with twitching whiskers, is close to what was once her shoulder but is now just part of the sloping mass of her rubbery moss-colored body. Georgia's antennae twitch as she takes in the rat's sleek apartment.

She slides away from the rat, whose hairless tail, so naked and thin, loops up from below and is clutched between his claws. When Georgia slips off the bed to the wooden floor, her small lower feelers graze a pair of striped boxers. A trail of slime grows behind her as she glides through the rat's place. She hooks her purse with a large antenna, and as she shuts the door behind her, she glimpses the whitish configuration that marks the floor like the chalk outline of some terribly misshapen body.

She inches down the stairs and wonders how she can possibly explain any of this to her husband. A rippling wave moves through her, and she feels the constricting of her new body as she slides forward.

On the street, no one looks twice, and Georgia wonders if her husband perhaps won't either. Her large antennae tremble, and she decides she'll go to the beach, a place she hates.

The gritty sand sticks to the mucus that coats what Georgia thinks of as her belly but is technically her foot. The slowness with which she moves is excruciating. In the cold waves that surround her quivering, viscous body, she waits for the salt to dissolve her.

SWAN DIVE

After an unsuccessful harvest, why did the farmer decide to try a career in music? Because he had a ton of sick beets! My children hate my jokes. But I'm a father. We're supposed to make these jokes. Part of being a good parent is how I think of it. And I am a good parent when I have my girls, which is only two weekends a month and five weeks in the summer. Each time, it's like we're starting over, like I'm in a foreign land where nothing works the way I think it will. I get nervous, tell jokes they hate, trip over things, get lost on the way to the pool, bump into walls. By the end of these weekends, I feel bruised and battered. After five weeks in the summer, I feel like I need a wheelchair.

Regardless of some of this bumbling around, I'm think I'm a decent dad. I take them to the public pool. I order pizza and Chinese food as a treat and cook the rest of the time. We watch bad movies that I let them pick. Last night, we watched a movie that's a modern take on Cinderella, and I wanted to tear out my eyeballs, but my three daughters sat rapt in front of the screen, hanging on to every inane word that came out of that tween princess's mouth. Maya is six and probably shouldn't be watching movies like this, but Leila and Sunny, my thirteen-year-old twins, always say they shouldn't have to pay for my and their mother's mistake. Yes, they're referring to Maya, but they insist she's in on the joke.

I wonder about that a lot. Being a decent dad, I mean. Is it a good sign my girls feel comfortable punching me—pretty hard—when I make a bad joke? That they see me as approachable enough to punch? My own father was cold and distant, and I like to think my daughters see me as more of a friend. A friend they sometimes punch. But I don't want them to think I'm trying too hard to be their buddy. After all, it's important that children know there are limits. It makes them feels safe is what I read somewhere.

I often wonder if they miss me when they're with their mother. It's not a question I can ask my twins, but Maya is young enough to be brutally honest about the fact that all she really needs is her mom. No, Papa, I don't miss you when we're at home, she says without any hesitation while we lounge at the public pool. She says this with a smile, her cheeks still full to bursting with baby fat. I'm glad, I say and squeeze her tightly, feel her giggle into my chest and then push away. She skips over to the wading pool and splashes under a spouting purple hippo. Her little body is strong as she windmills her arms through the spray. Across from us, I watch the twins jump and dive from the highest diving board. I cringe as they arch their long, thin bodies, all skin and bone after their most recent growth spurt. They choreograph swan dives and flips, flinging their elastic bodies backward, stretching their arms behind them, and arrowing into back dives that slice the surface of the water. They jump, dive, and flip without hesitation, as if they know something I don't, as if somehow, no matter how they fall, they'll land safely.

ZERO-SUM GAME

A is for admiration, which is what you want from him more than anything. To inspire wonder is your goal, but you get the sense that you're failing miserably.

B is for beautiful, which is what he calls you, cradling your face between his hands, trailing his fingers up your legs. Lately, he throws it out in an offhanded way like "Hey, beautiful" when you walk by him at a party you attend together, where he spends the majority of the night huddled in a corner talking with a woman whose lithe body is barely covered by a flowery romper, which is somehow the style of the summer. She's like some kind of oversized baby, you think as you watch them. Some kind of hot giant baby.

C is for cunt, a word he likes to use a lot when you have sex, which embarrasses you, but you don't say anything because God forbid you come off as overly sensitive. He doesn't refer to you as a cunt or anything like that, but the first time he says this cunt is mine, you have to press your face in the mattress to stifle your laughter.

D is for desperate, which is how you're feeling these days.

E is for the embarrassment you know he sometimes feels because he is twenty-one years older than you. E is for explaining, which he does a lot, about work, food, travel, clothing. When you call him a mansplainer, he sulks for a few minutes and then explains why he isn't one.

F is for fickle, which you both are to a fault. Each time you meet, you're not sure who he'll be or who you'll try to be—for him, yourself, whoever is watching.

G is for generous, which he is with his money, his things, both of which he has in abundance. The trip to St. Kitts, the earrings, the Vespa he buys you so you can zip from campus to his place instead of walking. That he hasn't yet noticed you never pierced your ears, too afraid of needles of any sort even now, is disconcerting. But you push it to the back of your head, like you push the earrings to the back of your dresser drawer.

H is for husband, which he once was to a woman named Laura.

I is for indignant, which is how you feel so much of the time and which you do next to nothing about.

J is for Jess, the name of his seven-year-old daughter whom you met once while working as a babysitter at a dinner party.

K is for what you text him when he tells you he can't bring you to a conference in San Francisco after all.

L is for lust and lost. You feel both every time you see him, and the one feeling only compounds the other.

M is for marriage, which he says is a mistake he'll never make again.

N is for no, which is what you first say when he asks you to dinner.

O is for omission. When you tell the story of how you met at a dinner party, for example, you omit the fact that you'd been hired to watch the children so the adults could eat and get drunk without interruption.

P is for pedo, which is what your friends call him.

Q is for questionable, which is how you would, if pressed, characterize most of your actions since you've met him.

R is for renegade, which is what he calls himself sometimes and which you try to omit from your memory. When he calls himself a renegade for starting his own law firm at thirty, you refrain from telling him that makes him about as far from a renegade as he can get.

S is for sex, which is what this is all about really, but you're fine with that.

T is for telling yourself what you need to tell yourself.

U is for understood, which is how you felt at the beginning when he talked with you about books and writing and art and listened to what you had to say.

V is for vacillate, which is what you do all day every day.

W is for wobbly, which is how you feel now—wavering and wishy-washy—when you used to be so sure of who you were.

X is for an unknown variable in an algebraic equation. X is what your relationship feels like—abstract, changing, a placeholder.

Y is for yes, which is what he says without hesitation when you tell him we should take a break. You thought he would say, "Why?"

Z is for zero, which doesn't mean *nothing* even if it's simpler to think it does. Whatever it was you had with him wasn't nothing. After all, the absence of something is a thing in and of itself.

ROCOCO

In paradise, the women's breasts are perfectly round and full of gelatinous substances, their lips pink and swollen, their foreheads smooth as glass and coursing with botulism. These women are all a certain version of beautiful. The men are overweight and sunburned, eyes bugging out of their heads as they tell you about their boats. Bloated bullfrogs.

In paradise, the sand is powdery soft, and the sea alternates between undulating turquoise swells and blue-black waves that crack the collarbones of tipsy vacationers attempting to bodysurf. There are members-only clubs where celebrities vacation and where, more and more often these days, Margot gets an invite. She lives full time in paradise, and for a while there she tried to live like she did back in the States: wrangling kids and schedules, cleaning and cooking. But the help is so cheap in Roco that by the end of the third month, Margot has a live-in nanny, Alejandra, who now does almost all of this for her. Margot's sister, Lily, brings up Alejandra almost every time they talk, which is often. "What's she doing now?" her sister asks. "Massaging your feet? Peeling your grapes?"

Margot doesn't pretend anymore that having live-in help is strange or makes her feel guilty. It's par for the course in Roco, and it just seems easier to give in to everything paradise has to offer. When Margot first moved to Roco, she and Lily had jokingly referred to it as Rococo. Lately, Margot's been contemplating new breasts. So, while Margot loves her sister more than almost anyone else in the world and can't wait to see Lily, who arrives in just a few days, there's a part of Margot that dreads sharing her life in paradise live and in person. Lily's visited once before, but it was soon after they moved to Roco, before Margot had met anyone. Before Alejandra had taken over. Mostly, it's Margot who travels back to the States to visit family. After all, as Lily, who teaches high school English, likes to remind her, Margot doesn't even work anymore.

Margot is aware of how comfortable she's become in this place. The ease with which she has turned over many of her old responsibilities to Alejandra still bothers her. Though she doesn't miss the drudgery of doing it all—the house, the food, the never-ending laundry, and of course, the kids, beautiful as they might be—it still feels a bit strange. It seems that her sensible Midwestern roots stubbornly remain, their rough, knotted rhizomes reaching out in the cold darkness, far beneath the white, hot sun.

In paradise, there's a saying: Staying more than five years is whack, and once you go whack, you can't go back. Gringos who stay longer are either criminals or lost. What's acceptable is going in, making bank, and getting out before the five-year mark. At least that's what most of Carlos's friends in Roco seem to be doing: developing real estate, building yet more hotels, and then heading back to the States. Carlos, her husband, was hired to design and oversee the construction of new vacation homes at Eldo, one of the private clubs. This is how Margot comes to be invited into the velvety fold of an obscenely wealthy group of women despite the fact she is not of their ilk.

Margot still struggles not to gawk when she's at her newish friend Ellen's house, where there is a room designated for gifts and gift wrapping. One night, while tipsy, Margot wandered in there and dizzily took in the rows of boxed Hermès scarves, tiny silver cups and spoons nestled in blue boxes, bohemian wrap bracelets glinting with slick, pale stones. She'd steadied herself on a stack of cashmere wraps. Just this past Thanksgiving, Ellen had hustled out of the gift room with two brand-new iPads, encased in brightly colored shatterproof grips, for Margot's children. Margot had protested that it was too much, and it really was, but her kids had seen the loot, and they howled and cried until Margot relented. Ellen is married to Carlos's boss and seems to have taken a liking to Margot, which makes Carlos very happy. Margot is confused by this friendship given that she and Ellen don't share a lot of common ground. But she is often lonely in Roco, the connection is good for Carlos's career, and Ellen is mostly fun. So, when Ellen dangles an invite in front of her, Margot is almost embarrassed by how gladly she snaps it up.

Beneath all that sun, beneath the swaying palm trees and the more and more frequent buzz of excellent champagne, Margot feels there might be something wrong with this place. It's not a pressing worry or need; it's that thing you know you should do, but you keep forgetting, so it sits there beneath the surface, and when it does briefly break through, you tell yourself you'll take care of it another day. On some level, Margot is always thinking, Tomorrow I'll talk to Carlos about a timeline, a real one. And technically, Margot always reminds herself, she and her family have only been in Roco for a year; they have almost four more years before they're too whack to go back.

* * *

Margot opens her eyes to see her son, Willie, leaning in, two inches from her face. His breath is hot, and, at four years old, it has just begun to carry a sour note in the mornings. She reaches for him and smothers her face in his cheeks, which are still so soft and full: cheeks of a toddler, breath of a man. He lets her pull him into bed with her and hold him, something she knows won't last much longer. If she draws letters on his back, he'll stay for a while. S-u-n, she writes across his tan skin. W-a-t-e-r.

Carlos is long gone, surfing before work, a ritual that cannot be fucked with. Born in Mexico, Carlos hated Chicago—the frigid gray winters, the unrelenting wind, the lack of an ocean. They'd lasted a mere year there before Carlos presented her with his plan and the job offer in Roco, though they'd spent seven years in Los Angeles, where his family had moved when he was in fifth grade. Carlos claimed the move to Roco was "a way to be closer to my roots—the children's roots too." True, he was born in Mexico, but he had moved to LA at such a young age. Sometimes Margot feels as if she'd been tricked by Carlos and his whole cultural roots spiel; Roco just seems like an extension of California but cheaper. "One year in Chicago in exchange for seven in Los Angeles, and now he's dragging you to Mexico? Seems fair." Her sister had turned away from Margot when she said this but not before Margot saw her tears. More than anything, it feels as if she has traded in her family back in Chicago, traded in her sister Lily, so that Carlos can surf again. When Margot talks with Lily, and her sister lists off the litany of things she has to help their elderly parents with, Margot can feel her sister's criticism radiate through the phone.

"Mama, spell!" Willie demands. Margot smooths her hand back and forth across his tiny shoulder blades, erasing the last word. She'd felt so alone in Roco that first year, her only connection to the outside was Carlos, and he'd spent so many hours at work, which was, of course, necessary. And then his insistence that any time he was free, she leave the kids with Alejandra and come watch him surf, the strange, irritating expectation that now that they had help, she could focus on him again—Look at me! Look at me!—as if he were another child.

The other night in bed, he'd cupped her breasts and sighed before kissing them and declaring them her "sweet, little boobies." Margot wasn't sure what she was most unnerved by: the sigh, his use of the word *little*, or his use of the word *boobies*. She can't stand when adults use children's language to describe anything, and it seemed particularly offensive in reference to her own body. It has crossed her mind more than once that perhaps Carlos is cheating on her—maybe with a woman who tolerates the baby talk. Carlos is different here somehow, a whiff of entitlement, something peremptory in his manner. A-h-o-l-e, she thinks. She doesn't, of course, trace this across her son's small, beautiful back, but she spells it out in her head.

Valentina, her six-year-old daughter, peers into the bedroom. She's tried to straighten her brown curls with water, but they spring wildly about. She hates her curls, seems affronted by their unruly nature. Valentina is more poised than most adults, and she is already dressed in her school uniform, everything neat and tidy, tucked, and ready to go. "Get up, Mama," she tells Margot. "It's time for school."

At the Montessori, the children are all from somewhere else. Valentina and Willie, American to the core but now nearly fluent in Spanish, proudly announce themselves as Mexican and American to anyone who asks. The children of the locals who make Roco run smoothly, the ones who keep it beautiful, go to the Catholic school or public school in Old Town, which sprawls up the hills on the other side of the Centro. Margot asked about the public schools when Carlos had made his bid for Rococo. She was a public school kid and prided herself on sending her kids to the school down the street from their place on the North Side of Chicago. Carlos laughed and told her it was out of the question in Roco, and anyway they could afford private with his new salary.

Margot watches her friend Ellen's kids hop out of a black Suburban with tinted windows and wave to their driver. A nanny is one thing, a driver something else entirely. Margot likes to tell herself that even if she and Carlos could afford a driver, they wouldn't hire one. She turns to her own children, strapped into the back seat, and watches Valentina dutifully unbuckle Willie. Margot recites what she does every time she drops them off: "I'll see you at two. Wear your hats when you're outside. Mama loves you." Her children walk through the school's arched entrance, Valentina clasping Willie's hand. How, Margot wonders, have I ended up with such good kids?

Because the thing is, Margot doesn't always think of herself as a good person. Not good in the same way as Lily, who can be so judgmental and critical but as a child was driven to rage by even a whiff of injustice. In grade school, Margot watched with wonder as Lily went after a girl who had lightly smacked an autistic kid on the head because he didn't understand the rules of a game. "He's not a dog," Lily screamed, grabbing the girl's long blond ponytail, twisting it around her palm and yanking so hard that some of the hair tore out in her fist.

Margot's not horrible, of course. She's kind most of the time and has empathy for others: she's no sociopath. But she can veer toward self-involved, and she feels herself pulled in that direction more and more these days. Carlos is the same but unabashedly so. She's embarrassed to remember that when they first met, it was something that drew them to each other—their ability to put their needs before others'. They called it independence and ambition. They called it knowing themselves.

At Eldo, Margot relishes the way her sister Lily's mouth drops open just a bit when they pass through the entrance, which comes out of nowhere, carved between two craggy rock outcroppings. A green canopy of palm trees and fuchsia bougainvillea ushers them forward to the guard station, discreetly housed in a moss-covered grotto. Margot often wonders how much water is used to keep this jungle-like entrance in bloom, so verdant and alive that it looks fake. Her first time at Eldo, she'd reached out to thumb some of the greenery, sure it would be waxy and plastic, only to feel the crisp split of a leaf bent between her fingers.

After a uniformed, smiling local finds her on the list, under Ellen's name, he takes her car keys and gives them the key to one of the club carts. The black iron gates swing open, welcoming them to the paradise within paradise. As they walk through the main club's entrance, Margot delivers a sharp elbow to her sister's ribs. "Look left," she whispers, tilting her head toward the patio where Melissa Barlow, movie star turned lifestyle guru, sits on the patio with two other women. Without hesitation, Lily replies, "Are you kidding me? That's the empress of kale! The queen of the tenderly steamed vagina!" Oh, how Margot loves Lily. She's been looking forward to bringing her sister here for months. The place is so ridiculously luxurious that Margot feels as if she's found the perfect gift for Lily: the gift of mercilessly and gleefully judging these people while taking advantage of all the perks they enjoy. While Lily might rail against injustice, she's not a saint.

Though Carlos works for the Eldo Corporation, they are not members of the club, membership depending, after all, on the ownership of one of the multimillion-dollar beachfront homes. Not in this lifetime. She's particularly excited to show Lily the "comfort stations"—little outposts full of booze, candy, and Froyo—that dot the golf course. She is still amazed by these comfort stations, there expressly to fulfill the sudden cravings of rich people playing golf but more often sitting empty of people and full of all that treasure. Whenever she comes home from an event at Eldo, Willie and Valentina race for her purse, which they know is filled with raided treats just for them. The first time Ellen rocketed their golf cart over to one of these stations, taking wild turns down the path so that Margot felt as if the cart might tip at any moment, adding to the dizzying effects of the champagne that sloshed about in her plastic flute, Margot had regressed back to childhood, gorging herself on nachos and frozen yogurt. Eldo is like summer camp: a gorgeous, lush, and strange summer camp for adults.

Ellen waves to them from across a pool that laps over an intricately tiled ledge gesturing toward the glimmering ocean. She is with Rajika, her Indian friend. This is always how Ellen introduces Rajika—as her Indian friend, never just her friend. Margot doesn't yet know these women well enough to make a joke about this. And the thing is, Ellen is funny and unbelievably generous, so when she says things like this, Margot pretends not to register it. Rajika has never said a word about being introduced as Ellen's Indian friend, so Margot just inwardly cringes every time Ellen does it and then cringes again when she's too chicken to point it out.

When Margot told Ellen that she herself is half Vietnamese, Ellen just laughed and said, "Get out. No, you're not." Margot takes after her father, who is white, a nose just like his, streaks of blond in her hair. It is not uncommon for people to react the way Ellen did; what's different, though, is that Ellen never asks Margot another thing about it. But once at a dinner party Ellen hosted, one of the guests, a venture capitalist who lives in San Francisco, started complaining about how many Asians live in the city. Ellen looked over at him and said without smiling,

"And you think they're excited to have overgrown frat boys like you, who all drive the same Land Rover and wear the same sneakers, living next door?" She looked over at Margot and winked right after she ripped into him.

When Ellen introduces Rajika to Lily as "my Indian friend, Rajika," Margot prays her sister will just let it slide but realizes that's likely impossible. Lily greets Rajika, and then leans conspiratorially toward Ellen and says, "So that must make Margot your Asian friend, huh? It's absolutely lovely to finally meet both of you." Lily delivers this with so much warmth and with such a large smile that it seems possible for Ellen not to register the dig. Confusion flashes across Ellen's face before she lets out a sharp laugh. "I thought Margot might be lying about the Asian thing, but now that I've met you, I can see it!" Ellen replies and then raises her hand in the air, signaling for drinks.

The women have guzzled two bottles of champagne, and Margot watches Lily absorb the conversation, which revolves around the kids' school, nannies, and second homes. Lily's dark brown eyes narrow now and again, but she seems to be enjoying herself. Margot's sister's shoulders, which usually hover scrunched up near her ears, a marker of tension and defense that is as familiar to Margot as Lily's raspy voice, are loose and low. Lily has settled back onto a lounge chair, her legs crossed before her, and her dark hair is spread out like a blanket against the immaculate white cushion. Often Margot is content to bask in the beauty of this place, half listening to conversations that have so little to do with her own life: ski condos in Sun Valley, apartments in New York. A woman named Lolo, who is part of Ellen's group, recently returned from a trip to Bali where she vacationed with the matriarch of a trio of TV stars famous primarily for their enormous butts and tiny waists.

But with Lily there, Margot is the one who can't seem to relax and enjoy herself the way she usually does, and she holds back on adding anything at all to the current conversation, as if she might blurt out what she imagines her sister must think of these women: *You are all dim and privileged big-breasted monsters.* Instead, she watches Lily take in Ellen's perfect physique, her long taut torso, her birdlike bones, and incongruously full breasts. Ellen has talked openly with Margot about the surgeries she's had—the "mommy makeover" after her two children—the replacement of one set of boobs filled with salty water for a new set filled with gel, "like gummy bears" is how she explained it to Margot. "Feel them," she'd offered, and Margot had barely paused before grabbing a handful. When she squeezed, they did indeed have a density and give similar to gummy candy.

"The city claims the sauna is too large and not in keeping with the architectural integrity of our neighborhood. The wood is from Sweden, for God's sake." "I'm sure there's a way around it": this from Rajika. "First-world problems, am I right?" Lily chimes in without missing a beat. Margot knows Lily loathes this catchphrase, as Margot's been audience to her sister's diatribe on the way her tone-deaf students use it. Margot braces herself for what's sure to follow because, for her sister, this must just be her opening gambit. But Lily leaves it at that, and Margot watches Ellen and Rajika throw back their heads in exaggerated laughter, their slender necks exposed.

* * *

The women pile into the golf cart, and Ellen zips them down paths that unfurl under palm fronds and roll past cactus gardens, orange and red blossoms bursting alongside razor-sharp spines. Lily is perched up front next to Ellen, a flute of champagne dangling from her fingers. Margot is buzzed enough to have relaxed into the rollicking atmosphere, and she feels proud of Lily, whose company Ellen and Rajika are clearly enjoying. Her sister is opinionated and sometimes too intent on making sure everyone in the room understands that she's smart, but Lily knows how to have a good time. Margot hears Rajika asking Lily about her teaching, listens to her sister's funny anecdote about which Shakespeare play her students hated most. Still, along with the pride Margot feels toward her sister, she feels something else too, something thrumming through her chest that she can't yet name. She swallows more champagne, and her stomach lurches as the cart careens around another corner.

Ellen must be lit because she drives the cart right up the sidewalk to the door of the comfort station on hole nine, crunching the corner of the front bumper in the process. Once again, she throws back her head and laughs. "Yikes" is all she says. Their little golf cart will be replaced with a new one, just like the endless supply of fluffy new towels that appear on the lounge chairs right after a dip in the pool, or the bounty of salads, fruit, shrimp, and steak that materialize before them on the ocean terrace. And never with any discussion or exchange of money. Every need and desire fulfilled without asking. The entire place, really, is just one big comfort station.

The women grab at single-serving bottles of champagne, mini whiskeys, handfuls of licorice, throwing some of this into their totes, pausing to open up bottles and take a swig. Rajika knocks over a jar of candies, which scatter across the counter like brightly colored little bugs, and Margot scoops up a few to toss back. Lily places a single tortilla chip under the nacho cheese dispenser and pumps a swirling mess of unnaturally orange cheese product on top. She blows out her cheeks like a chubby kid for Margot, who she knows is watching, before she stuffs the whole thing in her mouth. Meanwhile, Ellen bends backward beneath the frozen yogurt dispenser, her impossibly lean body held at an angle achieved by hours of Pilates and stomach crunches. Rajika pulls the machine's handle, releasing dollops of yogurt, most of which miss Ellen's mouth and land on her chin and neck, before dribbling to the floor. Small mounds of vanilla have already started to melt and pool on the polished tile. After a few minutes Ellen unbends her rubbery body, towels the yogurt off her face and chest, and then drops the towel to the floor. "Ughhhh. I need to either shower or swim. Let's go."

"Hold on." Lily is swiping the counter beneath the nacho dispenser, wiping up drips of cheese. She moves to another counter and cups one hand beneath the edge while using the other to sweep spilled candy into it. Margot bends to brush together some of the candy on the floor, and Ellen kicks lightly at the small pile she's managed to gather so that the candy goes skittering beneath the countertops. "Just leave it. It's fine."

Lily continues to tidy up the mess they've made, and when she gets to the yogurt machine, she waits for Ellen to step aside. Margot knows that Ellen isn't going to move, just as she knows that her sister wants to start something. Lily and Ellen stand facing one another, just a few inches apart, and Margot's stomach drops as she feels for just an instant that she can see inside both these women to the rigid core of who they are, what keeps them facing each other, ramrod straight without any intention of giving in to the other. "You're aware that someone else is going to have to clean this up, right?" Lily is looking at Ellen and doesn't seem angry, more curious as to whether Ellen understands this to be the case. Ellen smiles widely at Lily, and then she brushes a handful of candies from the counter to the floor. "Of course, I know that someone will have to clean this up because there is a person here whose job it is to clean this up."

Margot knew it wasn't possible for this night to end without Lily lecturing someone on something. In fact, she realizes she's been waiting for this all night, realizes that part of what bothered her earlier wasn't just that Lily might say something offensive, but that her sister hadn't been reacting to these women in the way Margot imagined she would. And what Margot admits to herself now is that she feared Lily's restraint came from seeing Margot as more similar to Ellen than to herself—the sisterly "us" no longer a given.

Margot feels an unexpected surge of fear mixed with pleasure course through her body as she waits for Lily to respond. But Ellen and Lily both look over at Margot expectantly, waiting for her to interject, to—she realizes—take sides. She is too slow, and Lily turns back to Ellen, steps around her, and begins to pick up the wrappers and corks littering the countertop. In response, Ellen reaches over to the yogurt machine and pulls hard on the handle, leaning into it so that the handle swings as far down as it can go, and a long rope of vanilla spools out onto the grate below the machine before it overflows and spills onto the floor. With her free hand, Ellen reaches into a jar of pastel nonpareils, grabs a handful, and tosses the candy up in the air like confetti. Rajika sits on the counter, her head flitting this way and that, from Ellen to Lily and back again, like a nervous bird.

Lily, who's tossing wrappers into the trash, first looks at the mess of rainbow candy skittering across the tiles and then lasers in on Ellen. It's clear to Margot that her sister, who does not have children, doesn't understand that Ellen, merely an overgrown child, albeit an overgrown child with money, power, and the right to vote, will not engage in a debate with her, will not verbally spar, that she's only capable of making yet more of a mess. "Come on, Ellen, that's just straight-up fucking wasteful." Lily delivers this with a jokey lilt, and she squats and starts to pick up candy from the floor.

The yogurt machine whirs and the creamy white mess at Ellen's feet begins its melting creep. Ellen leans back on the counter behind her, like she's settling in for the night shift, and her skinny but well-muscled arm looks like it could pull down on that lever for eternity. When Lily walks over to Ellen, she doesn't pause before cocking her own arm and slicing down on Ellen's, right at the crook of her elbow like Margot's son Willie strikes at a board in Tae Kwon Do class. An ugly screech escapes Ellen's mouth, but she quickly composes herself. She looks over at Margot with disgust and says, "You know you'd be fine with this if she"—Ellen jerks her head toward Lily—"weren't here judging you." Ellen delivers this with the glassy cool tone Margot's used to and then struts out of the comfort station, Rajika following quickly behind.

"I was going to do something," Margot says to her sister.

"I know you were," Lily replies too brightly.

Margot's face grows hot, and there is a twist of panic in her chest as she considers this lie from her sister, the first of which has ever been aimed at her. There is relief that follows her panic now that Margot understands, completely, who she has become, and she lets it wash over her as she watches her sister crouched on the floor, wiping up Ellen's mess.

WINTER WITCH

We gather birch, eastern hemlock, and white pine for the pyre, which rises like a long, bony finger from the rocky shore at the tip of the peninsula, itself a knobby digit jutting out into the depths of a sprawling bay. A finger upon a finger, pointing heavenward. Accusatory.

We will light the pyre at three minutes after the stroke of midnight, and its monstrous blaze will burn out the Winter Witch and usher in the longer days of spring and then summer. A blaze that will summon the sunlight that weaves through cherry orchards, skips sharply across the surface of the water, a pale glassy blue in some places, bruised indigo in others.

With the endless warm summer days comes the long line of summer people, snaking a path up from the city.

We watch them as they gather their lanterns beneath the festive, twinkling lights of the town green. They can't see us in the darkness of the woods that ring the beach. At midnight, they will release their lanterns like so many globular jellyfish. Iridescent orbs will float against the night sky until the paraffin burns out and the lanterns swish back down to earth, their paper shells and bamboo skeletons happened upon for months after summer's end.

We listen to them count down. The cheers from the crowd unfurl into the night as the lanterns catch the wind and sail up, like full, rounded bellies lit from within. And that's when we douse the pyre in gasoline, toss the book of matches, dance as the hiss and roar of fire cracks across the shore, echoes out onto the water. The pyre will burn big and fast, the dry white pine already starting to smolder in places. The pine burns fastest, sharpens the scent of the woods around us. Tomorrow, only a few charred pieces of wood and piles of ash will remain. By week's end, the burned remnants will have tumbled this way and that, the ash carried aloft by the wind.

What the city people don't know is this: We are the Winter Witch, and when we light that pyre, what we are really doing is exorcising our desire—heightened and active all winter—to drive them off our lands. We convince ourselves that we do not wish to invade their summer houses in the dead of winter to light fires in their hearths, or to run our fingers over the soft leather of the living room couches on which we sometimes nap.

We tell ourselves that we did not, would not, close in on the Brockler place—so large and white with pine green shutters up against the vast array of windows. We would not jump the fence of the riding ring at the back of the property and move as if in unison, like a pack, across the wide expanse of the snowy lawn. How would we know that the Brockler place is checked only three times each winter by a caretaker from the city, or that for all the money the Brockler family has, they still won't pay for a security system or tip more than twelve percent?

How could we know how cold and beautiful it is in the house, or that thick oriental rugs cover the wood floors and feel plush beneath socked feet? We would fall back on the beds to test their springy pillow-top mattresses. We would not open the pantry and laugh at the amount of store-brand canned beans and vegetables the Brocklers have stockpiled. We would never go down to the cellar and select a bottle of wine from what must be at least two hundred.

We do not recall a time we threw back the cover of the dining room table and found our places around the still polished and gleaming mahogany surface, a time when we uncorked the wine and filled the cut crystal goblets taken from the rosewood hutch, a time when we raised our glasses and delicately clinked across the table. Nor do we recall starting a fire in the fireplace that rises like a stone tower on one side of the living room. But flames we remember, growing taller and brighter as we gathered around them, drinking then dancing, glad for the way the warmth spread from within.

PERSPECTIVES

I remember that summer at the beach, my favorite one-piece swimsuit, mango yellow with deep scoops in the front and back. You next to me, an arm thrown over your eyes, bottles of sunscreen strewn around you. Your pale body fleshy with curves, mine burned brown, flat and two-dimensional.

I remember listening to a group of boys a few feet over, one asking the other, "Why is a girl in a bikini like chicken?" His stupid laugh as he delivered the punchline: "'Cause the white meat is the best part." Idiot, I remember thinking. Everyone likes the dark meat better. That summer we decide to buy our first bikinis.

I remember the deep blue of the endless water and sky. The hours of summer endless too. I remember so much talking. Always talking. If not in person, then on the phone. Late into the night in the twin beds of your bedroom. But what did we talk about other than boys and the girls we hated? I don't remember. Never your father.

I remember glimpses of him in a hospital bed in your den. Peeking over at him when we ran up the stairs to your room. One day he called out to us, and he was wearing red wax lips. Your little brother next to him, laughing behind his own waxy pair. Your father was bald, his face bloated from the chemo, and with those giant red lips, I found myself repulsed and afraid and then guilty because I knew you were watching your father die a little bit more every day of that summer.

I remember getting drunk for the first time in your bedroom, your mother too busy taking care of your father to notice. I remember rolling on your shag carpet and getting my braces caught in the wormy threads, yelling at you to find scissors to cut me loose.

I remember the day your mother called us at my house and asked for you. You stood in my bedroom listening to her, and I looked past you at the trees in my backyard, at the falling leaves, the gray sky. It was homecoming weekend of our first year in high school. There was a football game we were headed to, but instead you went home to your father's dead body.

I remember watching you throw dirt on your father's coffin after they lowered it into the ground. You didn't cry. I remember how ready you were to move on. But in the years to come, it seemed that nothing would go right for you, that instead of moving on, you were stalling out. And I remember thinking that if you just put your mind to it, you could get through high school, college, the jobs that came afterward. If you just worked hard, you could do anything you wanted. I realize now that a person can't will herself into happiness and productivity. I realize now that I knew nothing of your grief back then, or the years that followed, because I was a girl who thought hard work solved any problem, and you were a girl who watched her father die.

NEUTRALITY

"Sexually, I'm inspired by Switzerland," he says to her over mediocre merlot in a sleek, dark bistro. As in later he'll be neutral about positions? she wonders. Or he'll remain silent and smiling afterward—polite but distant? Perhaps what he means has nothing to do with not making choices or bold pronouncements. Maybe he means he'll wind her up expertly, her body a sleek Piaget? Or he'll melt, stir, and stretch her like the fondue the Swiss are famous for? Who would say something so stupid about sex?

He takes a big swallow of wine, swishes it around in his mouth so dramatically that it looks like he's gargling it. Ahhhhhhh, he exhales so forcefully that she feels his breath on her face. Some of them are like this—brash, classless, gauche. But many are not. Most of her clients are unfailingly polite and reserved, but not because they're nervous; not one of them is ever nervous. Their reserve seems more like a projection of self-assurance, their knowledge that in almost any given situation, they are more powerful than the people who surround them; they have nothing to prove, feel no need to perform confidence.

She spends her evenings guiding these men through conversation, performing her interest in what they say, what they do, what they like and dislike, then sleeping with them and offering a performance of a different kind. She isn't troubled by what she does. She makes more money doing this than any other job she has ever had. She has a B.F.A. in painting and has worked as an assistant to a higher-ranked assistant to the curator of more than one gallery. Those jobs and this one have some commonalities: At the galleries, she had mostly smiled and listened to her bosses perform interest in their clients' opinions on art, enthusiastically agreeing with whatever a buyer said, no matter how stupid. The men who came into those galleries were similar to the men she spent time with now. Of course, there is one key difference between those jobs and this one, but she makes almost ten times as much doing this than she did as a gallery assistant. She also has a lot more time to paint. Win-win is how she thinks about it.

His car is expensive and quiet, as if it runs on air and hovers above the road. They all drive cars like this—sleek, silent, and fast, like a cheetah that sprints after a gazelle, or a shark that slices through the water after a seal. She runs her hand over the soft leather seat beneath her. He talks about the car as they drive to his hotel—how much it cost, how difficult it is to acquire one, about the trip he took to Italy to visit the factory where it was made. "I drove one of their race cars around a professional track," he tells her, and she thinks of her nephew, who is three and obsessively runs his Matchbox cars along counters, up walls, across furniture. "That sounds amazing," she tells him. The man looks over at her, beaming, and then places his hand high up on her thigh and squeezes. She places her hand over his, squeezes it lightly, smiles, and says, "Tell me more."

REFLECTIONS

At the train station, the platform is as crowded as usual. A mother pushes a stroller down and back, down and back, as the baby wails with what seems like righteous anger. *How dare you strap me in this thing and make me wait.* The poor child is splotchy from crying, and the young mother bends next to the stroller, offering up pacifiers and plush toys, squeaking this and that in the baby's face, with a smile sliced across her face. The young mother's back aches right beneath the clasp of her bra, and she stops to arch and stretch her spine, which feels hooked from bending over the stroller, the crib, or the blanket for tummy time, which always makes the baby miserable, all screams and spit-up. When she U-turns the stroller for the fifth time, her eyes meet those of an older woman sitting on a bench, who has been watching this show since it started. The old woman's lips curl up into a tentative smile, and the mother feels her own quiver.

On the last drive-by, the baby seems to have given up, the wails gone to hiccupping breaths. The old woman on the bench wants to offer the baby's mother a seat, a cocktail, another set of arms, a massage, a chair in a room that is utterly still and silent. The mother looks over, catches the gaze of the woman on the bench, and glares at her. *It gets easier*, the older woman wants to say to the young mother. But does it? Really? In some ways yes, but as her children grew, their problems grew too. So, it would be a lie to say it gets easier. Rather, it becomes a different kind of difficult, punctuated by periods of joy, happiness, and success, of course. But it is always difficult, she thinks. The worry never stops no matter that her children have grown and have lives of their own. Always love, yes. Fierce love shadowed by worry. She had learned to live with this coupling of love and worry, understood that this is how it would be. Always.

LOIN PRODUCT

There were signs to which she turned a blind eye. The droopy mustache that he called *ironic.* "You grew it, didn't you?" she'd asked. "There's nothing ironic about that." He'd sulked and stroked his whiskers. His muttonchops, also ironic according to him, gave her another momentary pause, but it was so much simpler to close her eyes and briefly wonder why hair was so easy for him and irony so difficult. Who was she to judge? Which was worse: wearing the *ironic* mustache or sleeping with the person who wore it?

When her face became oddly puffy and bagels made her gag, she peed on a stick and showed it to him. "Don't get me wrong," he said. "I could get behind some loin product at some point." She watched his lip stretch across his teeth as he talked, watched the coarse hairs above it twitching and settling. When he dropped his eyes, she kept looking at him.

She lies back on the table, and all she can think of is his term *loin product.* How disgusting it is. She is reminded of Humbert Humbert's ode to Lolita: *Light of my life, fire of my loins. Lo-lee-ta: the tip of the tongue taking a trip of three steps down the palate to tap, at three, on the teeth.* But the lines from the novel have been ruined now; she slips and trips over it again and again, *fire of my loin product.* And then it's over. She sits up and tries to listen to the nurse who gives her aftercare instructions. She runs her tongue over her front teeth, bites the tip of it until she tastes blood.

BUNNY

1

The rabbits come in dozens, it seems. Nothing one minute, invasion the next. They crouch in the grass like tiny statues, gray fur flecked with white. Cottontails. Leaf-ears at attention. Waiting. Kits, short for kittens—now called bunnies, as if *kitten* is not cute enough for the tiniest of these rabbits. Bunny, diminutive of the Scottish *bun*, a nickname for a pet rabbit. Also, slang for a young, attractive woman. She's a real bunny. A male rabbit is a buck, a female a doe. Before mating, the buck chases the doe until she turns and boxes at him with her front paws. They crouch and stare at each other. Face off until one or the other leaps into the air. Leap, leap, leap, come together.

2

No matter how long I sit on the back porch watching, I've never seen any of the rabbits mate. Yet there are so many of them dotting my yard like some kind of Disney movie. Bunnies hop through the grass, nibble and twitch, go still as stone when birds dive-bomb the shrubs. My child, who is too sensitive, who moves worms off the sidewalk and carries stink bugs outside, tells me that a female rabbit can produce up to ten litters a year, with up to twelve bunnies in each litter. Sometimes the mother eats her litter if she is stressed and fearful of predators, or she just eats the runt because it's going to die anyway. My daughter tells me all this matter-of-factly, like a little old woman familiar with the cycle of life, rather than the ten-year-old that she is. I feel a phantom elbow or foot punch me from within, the ghost of an ache low in my abdomen.

3

Giving birth can be painless, and it can be full of pain. It can be easy or difficult or anywhere in between. You can give birth in a sterilized hospital room or in a kiddie pool in a living room to the dulcet voice of your doula or midwife. You can give birth in the back of a car, on a bathroom floor, in a field, in an elevator, on the side of the road, in a mall, a forest, a library, an airplane, at prom, or in a grocery store parking lot. The list goes on and on and on. While giving birth, you may say or hear the following: birth plan, epidural, fuck, breech, Pitocin, I don't want this, breathe, I'm sorry, push, no, in distress, crowning, don't touch me. You may not hear or say any of these things. But at the end, you will have a baby, or you won't, and what you feel will depend on which.

SHE WASN'T

Her hair was not the platinum blond of a 1950s movie idol, or as black and shiny as onyx. Her eyes weren't cerulean or the warm brown of a doe. Her legs weren't muscled like an Olympian's or as slender as reeds poking up through the glassy surface of a pond. She didn't talk enough, or she talked too much. She wasn't tall, and she wasn't short. She wasn't humble or ambitious enough. She wasn't a mother—not even a godmother. She wasn't trilingual, ambidextrous, or double-jointed. She was unable to trill her *R*s or do the splits. She wasn't a professional mourner or a supertaster. She wasn't able to fly or breathe underwater. She wasn't a shapeshifter or a ghost. She was not all things magic and light, and she would not do.

THAT BABY

When Robert came into the bar with Naomi, they had between them a baby, maybe two years old. The baby wore what looked like one of Robert's undershirts, which billowed around him, the bottom of it sweeping his chubby ankles. Gayle had heard about her brother Robert's grandkid. People in town had taken to calling it "that baby of Cherry's" or just "that baby." This was the first time she'd seen the baby.

Robert and Naomi drove into Ely from McGill every couple of weeks, not so much to see Gayle as to sit at her bar and drink for free while they elaborated on their plans to move down to Vegas. Gayle had heard versions of this plan every time she'd seen them for the past four years, and she'd stopped encouraging them to go. McGill was rated "Most Economically Depressed Town in Nevada" by the Nevada Chamber of Commerce just the year before, and Gayle figured if that wasn't going to jump-start their move to Vegas, nothing would.

Robert and Naomi swung the baby between them as they walked, and the child squealed, his mouth wide and wet between cheeks like two fat peaches. The couple looked pale and brittle next to the baby, dried husks of corn. They swung him high, his feet swaying above their heads. The baby laughed with delight, and the cooing seemed to encourage them to swing faster and higher. Gayle cringed as she imagined the sharp pop of a little shoulder socket sprung loose. She tensed up as if in a moment she might be expected to catch the baby, flung accidentally from the careless hands of his grandparents.

Robert sat the baby on the counter in front of Gayle, who was tending bar. The diaper crinkled and squeaked over the Formica as the tiny boy dug his dirty heels in and tried to scoot himself over to the mess of straws, napkins, and ashtrays piled up at the edge of the bar. Gayle remembered the way her daughter, Kate, used to scoot herself around the kitchen the same way. She felt her body tense up as if at any moment the child might scoot himself off the counter and into Gayle's arms. Kate was now an adult and had long ago left town, and what Gayle remembered most about her babyhood was the low-level anxiety that surrounded her when Kate first attempted the most basic of things: sitting up, crawling, and those wobbly first steps. Everything about pregnancy and early motherhood had scared Gayle. Nothing felt natural, and she'd felt guilty about that. Guilty that she'd hated the strangeness of pregnancy, guilty that she'd been overcome with sadness in those first few months of Kate's life. Now she realizes that she'd had postpartum depression—but she was so young when she had Kate, she'd just assumed she wasn't a natural mother. It was Mel who took to parenting like a pro: nothing fazed him—not the crying, the projectile vomiting that plagued baby Kate until she got on solids, not the lack of sleep, the minuscule fingernails that needed clipping, the weigh-ins that made Gayle hold her breath as she prayed Kate was gaining weight what with all that vomit. What Gayle remembers most about that time is the overwhelming fear she felt all that first year. She remembers how much she looked forward to

6:00 P.M. when she and Mel would each have a beer before dinner.

The baby's cheeks were red from sunburn or rash, and in places his blond hair tangled into little clumps, like he'd been in burrs. The child looked up at her; his eyes were glassy and blue. Something that looked like dried mustard caked the bottom of his chin. Underneath the grime was the kind of face baby food companies wanted plastered across jars of pureed carrots and peas. The child let out a bored-sounding sigh and grabbed at his toes, still staring at Gayle.

"Gayle, meet Tin." Robert grabbed one of the baby's fat little hands and thrust it toward Gayle, who lightly grasped the boy's soft, warm hand with the tips of her fingers.

"Hey, baby." Gayle leaned on the counter to look the baby in the eyes. The baby smiled, his tiny teeth pearling up through pink gums.

"Tin?" Gayle asked Robert and Naomi, who sat leaning against the counter. Their hands formed empty circles waiting to be filled with whatever Gayle would give them.

"Cherry said she liked the sound of it."

"Cherry is crazy," Naomi piped in and sipped from the bottle of beer Gayle had set down in front of her. The only thing Gayle had ever heard Naomi say about Cherry was that she was crazy. Or ungrateful. Gayle wondered what Cherry had to be grateful to Naomi for. The baby smacked his palms down on the counter as if demanding a drink, and Naomi pushed a straw at him.

Gayle's husband and daughter had been after her to quit drinking for as long as she could remember, but she hadn't: not when Kate moved to California after high school and not when Mel followed her there three months later. That was two years ago. Gayle had let them go almost easily.

After they left town, Gayle had stepped up her drinking. She'd never been a volatile or sloppy drunk—never cheated on Mel or hit Kate. Instead, she'd treated them as if they were strangers, let Mel do all the parenting Kate needed, which wasn't a lot—her girl had always been independent. When Kate and Mel left, there was no reason for Gayle to pretend she had her drinking under control. And it had been a relief, really, when they left and there was no more pretending. For a while she'd felt more alive than she had in years. She'd been at least a little careful about her drinking, circumspect and cautious when Mel and Kate were still around. At the bar, she'd tip back with customers, but she still had to run her place—passed on to her from her parents when they died. At home, she'd start drinking at dinner and would stop when she fell asleep on the couch in front of the TV. This would happen to a cacophony of sighs and bedroom doors shut heavily—Mel had long ago given up lecturing her, but he registered his anger in his own small ways. Kate was gone long before she officially left home: forever at a friend's house or behind her bedroom door, always closed.

But when Mel and Kate had really left, she'd taken to staying at her bar and drinking after the night bartender took over. There wasn't much change in Gayle when she was drunk; she didn't get loud or flirtatious. What happened to Gayle was something small and wondrous. When she was drunk, she felt calm. Content. She didn't question herself and what she'd done or not done in Nevada, for her husband and daughter, with her parents' bar. She simply was. At times, the drinking brought Gayle bright bolts of possibility and hope that she'd become a different sort of person, that her daughter would look at her in some other way than as a stranger. She wasn't fooled by her sobriety once she found it: If she'd been able to sustain this feeling, this strange combination of contentedness and hope, she'd have kept on drinking forever. But like anything else that someone does for kicks, for relief, for the rush of happiness or possibility, it took more and more, and the feeling became increasingly elusive until it was finally gone.

Last year, the day after Kate's birthday, she'd quit. It wasn't something she planned; it wasn't that she'd talked to Kate or Mel and decided to finally clean up. She'd simply lost those moments of elation, that feeling of contentment. One day, she'd opened the bar and was washing glasses, looking at her hands, the bony knuckles and cracked skin, the chipped nails. They didn't seem a part of her, as if she had nothing to do with them at all. The longer she stared down at them, the more she felt like she had nothing to do with herself, with the physical body that stood behind a counter pouring drinks for her customers and herself. She was somewhere else, floating around outside her body, up near the ceiling fan.

That's when she checked into the hospital in Elko. She spent a month there detoxing, an utterly humiliating combination of watching her body turn on her and hearing herself explain how and why she'd arrived at this place in her life. When she got back home, Gayle figured if she could stay sober at her bar, she could stay sober anywhere. When she'd been sober for more than a year, people stopped taking bets on when she'd fall, and they stopped making the jokes about the bartender who wouldn't go near a drink except to serve it.

Robert and Naomi rattled their bottles against the counter, and Gayle replaced the empties. Naomi had set the baby on the floor, and Gayle watched him trundle over to the wooden Indian she had standing by the door. The bar's motif was Western: pictures of cowboys, teepees, and horses. It had once been a stop on the Pony Express, and Gayle's parents had decorated accordingly. Old black and whites of the messengers on their horses were framed on the walls, and a pair of saddlebags hung above the bar.

Gayle talked to Mel every once in a while, but he'd moved on from her. She hadn't talked to Kate since she left, though she'd sent Gayle three postcards with cryptic one-line messages. She knew that they were the only form of communication Kate was interested in at the moment. The first card Kate had sent her was a picture of a scarecrow, dried grass and corn husks sticking out from its knotted-off shirt and ripped jeans. Its head was a stuffed pillow slip, violently tilted to the right with a scare face painted across it—a big *V* between the two eyes and a mouth that turned down in a grimace. Next to it, a girl of about ten stood imitating the scarecrow: her arms splayed out at her sides, her head jerked to the right, her eyes narrowed, and her lips drawn down. She wore a red-checkered dress and no shoes. Written on the back in Kate's neat handwriting was one phrase: *To memories.* Gayle both dreaded and wished for the arrival of these postcards. She understood that the cards were born out of anger and sadness more than anything else, but Gayle also understood that it was better to get anger and sadness than nothing from her daughter. The cards seemed to herald the possibility of something more one day.

The afternoon customers were starting to come, and Gayle glanced questioningly toward the baby.

"Oh, he won't bother anyone," Naomi said. "He's as quiet as a mouse. Hasn't even said his first word yet, and he's almost two. Not a peep, Cherry says."

"Kid needs to be checked out, if you ask me." Robert looked over at the baby, who was poking at the wooden Indian's feet with his straw. "He's cute though, huh?"

"Where's his mother?" Gayle asked.

"I think she made a trip up to Reno. Something to do with his daddy, I guess. She didn't really say. We came into town to stay with the baby."

Gayle wasn't sure that Cherry hadn't completely lost her mind. Robert and Naomi weren't fit to take care of a cactus. She opened a packet of crackers, took them over to the baby, and squatted to hand him one. The baby gnawed on the edge of it, his fist balled around it so that half the cracker crumbled onto the floor.

"Has he eaten yet?" Gayle called over to the bar. Naomi and Robert didn't answer her; they were engrossed in conversation with some of the locals who came in at lunch. Robert had helped himself to a third beer. Gayle reached for the baby, waiting for him to screech or squirm at her touch. But Tin let himself be scooped up without a sound. He settled against Gayle's side and craned his neck around, surveying the room from his new position. Tin reached for the longhorns mounted above the door, and Gayle lifted him up so he could touch them. The child ran his hand, stubby and perfect, over the dry, chipped bone. He did it gently, with concentration, the way some kids pet a cat that others would bat or squeeze. The baby slapped his palm lightly on Gayle's shoulder when he'd had enough of the horns.

"Have you fed him yet?" Gayle set the baby on the counter by Naomi and Robert.

"Baloney. Tin loves it, don't you, baby?" Naomi squeezed the baby's little toe, and Tin pulled both his feet in toward himself, grasping them in his hands. Smart kid, Gayle thought.

"Is that the baby I've been hearing about?" Rick from the Chevron station leaned back on his stool to get a look at Tin.

"That's him," Robert said with a certain touch of pride that surprised Gayle. She never would have taken her brother for a doting grandpa.

Rick walked over to the baby and tickled him under his dimpled chin.

"I don't believe the little guy can do it." Rick looked over at Robert and Naomi. Gayle didn't like the echo of a dare she'd heard in Rick's comment.

"Oh, he can do it," Robert replied and grinned down at the baby.

Gayle watched her brother light a fresh cigarette off his old one and hold it out in front of the baby's mouth. The baby leaned forward a little bit; the neck of Robert's undershirt hung off his small, round shoulder, down to his elbow. He puckered his lips around the filter and waited, fists in his lap, for Robert to pull the cigarette out. The baby let out a wide rush of smoke and smiled. No sputtering or coughing, just a stream of smoke. Rick roared and slapped Robert on the back. Robert and Naomi clapped and grinned at the other customers who had gathered around the baby. Tin clapped his hands together and laughed, a wet gurgle of a laugh, encouraged by those around him. Gayle grabbed the cigarette from Robert's hand before he could offer the baby another drag. Gayle had pretty much known it would come to something like this when she saw the two of them walk into the bar, swinging the baby between them. She picked up the baby and backed away.

* * *

Gayle didn't have to twist any arms to get the baby. Naomi and Robert had friends to visit and wanted to hit Little Patch Casino while they were in town. They'd planned on taking Tin with them but seemed more than glad to leave him with Gayle.

Outside, the dry afternoon heat hit hard, and Gayle squinted in the bright sunlight. Tin turned his head to look over Gayle's shoulder as if he longed to return to the dark coolness of the bar. He didn't squirm or cry; he just sat in the crook of Gayle's arm as if used to being toted around by strangers. When Kate was a baby, she'd have screamed if anyone besides Gayle or Mel even so much as looked at her. Across the street, Gayle saw Patty, who owned the coin laundry, peering out her door. Gayle waved and then jiggled the baby since she knew Tin was the only reason Patty had gotten up from the orange plastic chair that seemed as natural a part of her body as her legs. She acted surprised, pretending she wasn't even looking right at Gayle before she waved back.

When Kate and then Mel had taken off to California, she'd gotten those same oblique glances from people all over town. She'd felt their eyes on her, but they always seemed surprised when she looked back, as if they'd been looking at a certain piece of blue sky right past her shoulder. Gayle stared back until they looked away—she knew what they were saying about her. Her drinking. Her inability to keep a man or even her kid, even though Kate was eighteen when she left and a legal adult. After about six months, people stopped staring, stopped wondering how exactly Gayle drove her daughter, and then her husband, out of town. It wasn't any secret in town that Gayle drank. But that wasn't the question. She knew they suspected there had been something else, something especially awful to top things off: cheating, neglect, maybe violence of some kind. But there wasn't. The truth—that her drinking had simply and steadily blotted out Mel and Kate—wouldn't have been enough. Gayle understood that what she'd done, or failed to do, for Mel and especially for Kate was wrong; she was reminded of it every day, everywhere she looked. And she took responsibility for it. But she was angry too—angry that what bothered these people most was that she was a woman, a mother, who'd failed her kid and her husband. Gayle understands that there is nothing worse to people than a bad mother. Had she murdered a customer, she would have been looked at with less judgment.

Gayle had come home from work one night to find Mel sitting in the kitchen. "She's gone, Gayle, and as soon as I get things in order here, I'm going too." He'd said it matter-of-factly, like it was a trip they'd been planning. She had always known Kate would take off as soon as she could swing it, and she hadn't ever tried to make it so she wouldn't. But Gayle had believed Mel incapable of leaving until the day he did. He'd been born just outside of Ely and going to Reno had been a big deal when she first met him. Now he was living in California, bartending at a TGI Fridays, and, judging from the way he would sometimes mention a woman named Jackie, was likely on his way to a second marriage.

Gayle hitched the baby higher up on her chest and crossed the street toward the Save More. The baby rubbed at his nose fiercely, so Gayle set the child on his feet, took a tissue out of her pocket, and knelt down beside him.

"Looks like you've got yourself a runny nose, huh?" She swiped at the baby's nose, pinching a little. Tin looked up at her dazed, slightly offended. Gayle was afraid the baby might cry.

"There you go. Better, huh?" Gayle smiled wide for the baby, hoping it would convince him there was nothing to cry about. Tin just rubbed his nose again and made for the street curb in an unsteady lurch, fast, like if he slowed down, he might lose his balance and fall. Gayle grabbed him and swung the child back up on her hip—it felt so natural. So easy. The fear she'd carried when Kate had been a baby felt as distant as the moon.

Broken glass, cans, and wrappers littered the curb. When Gayle had first moved out to Ely, the town had barely existed: just a few stores and bars, places the ranchers frequented. Now it was an oasis of fast-food restaurants, gas stations, quickie marts, and motels. Tin whimpered softly and pointed to a dirty yellow tennis ball that lay among the litter by the curb.

"We'll get you something better, okay?"

Gayle looked at the baby as if he might answer.

* * *

Inside the store, Gayle pushed the shopping cart past the aisles, peering down each one for diapers. She settled on a big plastic bag of Huggies and added a bottle of powder and some lotion, a drop of which she rubbed into the bumpy redness that spread across Tin's cheeks. The baby bounced around in his seat, squeaking and swiping at Gayle's hands for the bottle of lotion.

Gayle slipped a small hooded jacket on Tin and threw the matching track pants into the cart. She sorted through a bin of cheap canvas kids' sneakers and coaxed a few pairs onto the baby's feet before she could find a pair small enough. It crossed her mind that somewhere in Cherry's apartment the baby had these things: diapers, powder, T-shirts, and shoes. But then he'd shown up at the bar in a diaper and Robert's undershirt. She offered Tin a lime-green Nerf ball, which he grabbed with his small, puffy hands.

"Looks like you got quite a handful there, Gayle." She looked up to see Patty staring down at the baby from behind her empty cart. She'd probably followed her, torn her fat ass from her plastic chair in the laundromat just so she could harass Gayle about the baby.

"He's easy enough." Gayle tried to push her cart forward, but Patty headed her off with her own cart.

"He's Cherry's baby, right?"

"That's what they tell me, Patty." Rudeness never worked with Patty, but it was habit.

"Well, he's a cute little guy." Patty heaved herself over to Gayle's cart and patted Tin on the head absently. The baby leaned forward as if to escape her, and Gayle wheeled the cart back a bit, so Patty couldn't keep petting him like a dog. "Where's your mama and daddy, baby?" She looked at Gayle.

"They're house hunting up in Reno," Gayle lied.

"House hunting, huh?" Patty gave Gayle a smile that made her want to plow her cart right into Patty—smash through her pillowy folds and pin her to the shelves of macaroni and quick spuds stacked behind her.

"Why you always worrying about other people's business, Patty? Especially when you already know it? You know as well as I do, this baby hasn't got any daddy around."

Patty started to open her mouth and then stopped. She wheeled her cart around and headed down the aisle a few steps before she swung back to face Gayle. She knew Patty wouldn't be able to leave without getting in a last word.

"Well, good luck, Gayle," she hissed at her. "You know how hard it is."

Gayle watched her leave and looked down at Tin, who was staring up at her with watery eyes. Three deep grooves marked his forehead, little worry lines, as if he knew that things were wrong in the world.

* * *

They drove out past the edge of town, past the little clusters of long one-story houses, boxes painted pale shades of yellow and green like lemon and lime sherbet. Gayle's house was out by the Lund ranch. Gayle and Mel had bought the place from the Lunds when they got married. It was bigger than she needed now, but when Mel and Kate had been around, it was a good fit. The baby stirred next to Gayle, rubbing his eyes, and sighing lightly.

"You tired, Tin?" Gayle looked at the baby in the rearview mirror, who turned his head and rested his chubby cheek against the car seat Robert and Naomi had shoved into her car before hightailing it out of town. Gayle had been surprised they'd even had one, given the cigarette stunt. "Huh, you tired? Sleepy? You know sleepy, right?" The baby closed his eyes and then opened them back up at Gayle. "That's right, Tin. Sleepy." She kept waiting for the baby to cry or fuss, make some sort of demand, but the child remained quiet. Gayle wondered if too many afternoons with Robert, Naomi, and Cherry had taught the poor kid that it would get him nowhere.

Outside, the late afternoon sun hovered over the road, and the sagebrush bent in the wind; a few, broken free, tumbled about. Gayle's truck passed through the jagged wedges of dusty red rocks. They weren't mountains or even hills: just walls of rock that rose up only so high, leftover slices of something bigger that had disappeared long ago.

She carried the sleeping baby inside, set him on the couch, and propped a few pillows to keep him wedged in. She'd wanted a smoke since the bar but had been afraid to smoke in front of Tin, as if the baby might ask her for one. Gayle went out to the porch and moved a chair by the window, so she could look in on Tin. Normally around this time, she would walk down the road to the Lund ranch and watch the ranch hands work for a while. Then sometimes she'd go up to the house and talk with Dan and Karen. Gayle watched the baby sleep, his little body taking up just one square of the couch. He slept with his arms thrown over his head, his plump legs propped up. When Kate was a baby, she'd slept on her back, her feet sole to sole so that her tiny legs formed a diamond. Gayle and Mel used to watch her, amazed that she could sleep that way. From where she was sitting, Gayle could see Tin's little potbelly rise and fall. The sun blazed closer to the Sierra Nevada. and Gayle wondered what her daughter was doing, somewhere on the other side of those mountains.

The wind swept across Gayle's yard and rattled the chimes she'd hung from one of the porch beams many years ago. In the distance, she could see the huge semis that came off the interstate for gas or food or so the drivers could get out and stretch. Most came out of California, heading east toward Omaha and Chicago. Maybe they'd even passed through the town Kate was living in. The last card she'd received from her had been postmarked Bakersfield, California.

Inside, Gayle glanced at the baby, who hadn't changed positions. She hated to think about those postcards, to look at the strange scenes on the front of them. But she kept them like souvenirs from a sunny vacation, pinned to the fridge by chipped magnets. The second card Kate sent her had a picture of a gigantic beached whale on the sand with a man standing by it to show just how huge the whale was. On the back she'd simply written: *Greetings.* The last one was a black and white of a field of oil derricks, tall, skinny steel structures jutting up into the sky. Standing on the ground between the rigs were men and women stripped bare, all bony elbows, knees, and rib cages—an artistic point Gayle knew was meant to be beyond her. On the back, Kate's neat, rounded script announced: *Home.*

Gayle tried to imagine what Kate felt when she'd picked out the cards and picked out those words; she could feel the anger, the sadness, the resentment. Her whip-smart daughter understood that now that Gayle was sober, now that she wanted to hear from Kate and to see her, there was nothing Gayle could do but look at these postcards and wonder. After the first card, Gayle had tried to get in touch with Kate. But Mel wouldn't give her

Kate's number; he said Kate knew she would ask for it and had told her father that just because she sent a postcard didn't mean she wanted to talk. Gayle had taken to waiting for her postcards and taking the scraps of information Mel volunteered. Maybe the last postcard was something more—a nod to where Kate would be staying for a while. Then again, it could be one hundred other things. Gayle looked over at the baby; Tin was sucking his thumb and staring at her.

"You hungry yet? Hungry?" Gayle motioned at her mouth, prompting the baby to answer her. The baby reached up and pulled his plump lower lip. "Hungry?" she asked again, and this time the baby murmured softly and very clearly mimicked Gayle's movements by lightly touching his small fingers to his mouth. "Let's get you some food then." Gayle picked up Tin, and the baby's wet diaper squished against her arm.

She changed the baby's diaper, brought him to the kitchen sink, and ran a damp towel over his face, neck, hands, and feet. Gayle tried to smooth out the tangles of the baby's wispy yellow hair, and then she zipped him into his new sweat suit and slipped on his tiny sneakers.

"Now you're ready to take on the world, huh? Just get some food in you, right?" She fed the baby some crackers with bologna on them because it was the only thing she knew the baby liked for sure. Gayle then tried out some applesauce on him, and the baby ate it obediently. She cut up an orange, and Tin sucked at the pieces, reaching for a new section every few minutes. Occasionally, he let out a soft babble—what sounded to Gayle like a "baaa" or a "biggle." Gayle wiped the juice that dribbled down Tin's neck and chin, caught the pieces of food that slipped out of his hands. The baby gulped at the cup of milk Gayle held to his lips, straining his small neck forward, his hands busy with a piece of orange rind.

Later, they headed down the driveway and up the road toward the ranch. Gayle thought Tin would get a kick out of seeing the sheep and horses. She walked slowly, pacing herself to the child's uneven steps. Gayle's back started to ache from stooping forward to hold his hand, so she swung Tin back up onto her hip, felt the warmth of his small body against her. The sun was red over the mountains, and Gayle pointed for the baby to see. "Sun." Tin pointed the way she did but didn't say a word. "And mountains. And over those, California. And the ocean." The baby kept pointing even when Gayle stopped.

The bottom of the sun grazed the tops of the mountains, and Gayle dipped her head quickly, stealing a sniff of the child's hair, remembering the scent—something milky and vanilla—of Kate's hair and skin when she was a baby. Dust swirled up in the wind now and then, and the child turned his head to Gayle's shoulder, pressing his nose in lightly. Gayle thought of waking up in the morning and attending to the baby: the diaper change, the scrambling of eggs for his breakfast, a bath. The fading orange of the sun stained the sky above them.

At the ranch, Gayle waved to the workers and held Tin near the fence so he could pet the horses. The baby reached, trying to get closer to the animals, and ran his hands down their noses gently like he knew not to scare them. Gayle thought of Cherry disappearing, taking off with the baby's father to some distant town, never to be heard from again. She imagined Robert and Naomi shaking their heads and agreeing that Gayle was the one who should take care of Tin. Mostly, she thought of Kate coming home to find her rearing a healthy baby boy. Her girl would sit on one of the kitchen stools, her feet hooked under the bottom rung. She would watch Gayle deftly feed little Tin scraps of chicken and baby spoonfuls of mashed potatoes, watch the child squeal and laugh, see how well Gayle cared for him.

Gayle tightened her grip on the baby. She shifted Tin so that he could run his small hands along one of the horse's manes. The animal stood still, patient, maybe enjoying the child's tugs. Tin stretched out for more, and Gayle watched him, listened to the light babble of pleasure that occasionally slipped from his lips, and wondered at all the things in her world that could still be true.

HOW TO BE YOUR MOTHER'S BEST DAUGHTER

1. Be humble, don't ask for too much, and don't ask questions.
2. Wear the French blouses with cap sleeves edged in lace when all the other girls dress in miniskirts and paint-spattered sweatshirts slung from their shoulders.
3. Nod your head but remain silent when she curses your father, your sisters, on the very rare occasion your brother.
4. Later, remain silent when she curses you.
5. Don't ask her what she means when she says you or your siblings "don't have enough Asian."
6. Study yourself in the mirror, though you suspect that what you look like has nothing to do with the Asian-ness your mother is after.

7. When she calls you at college, just say yes when she asks if you're being moral. If you must, let the phone dangle from its cord and go into the hallway to talk with your friends. She will still be talking when you return.
8. Try to understand that she means well.
9. Don't have the third glass of wine at dinner with her even if you really want it.
10. Visit her at least three times a year, and when you do, fetch the green onions from the crisper and the rice from the pantry, slice the pork belly, chop the onions, dice the peppers, stir the soup.
11. Request the recipe.
12. Watch her curl her hand into a loose fist and bat it against her legs when she gets nervous.
13. Remember watching your grandmother, her mother, do the exact same thing while pacing the confines of a small one-room apartment on the outskirts of Paris.
14. Tell your husband not to be alarmed when, after your wedding vows conclude, your mother hugs him tightly and whispers in his ear, "I ask only one thing: Never get divorced."

15. Do not under any circumstances get divorced.
16. If you decide to have children, don't be offended when she says she needs only three things from you:
    a. That the child is given a normal name (your father's*).
    b. That the child is baptized.
    c. And finally that the child is circumcised.*

    * *If it's a girl, replace your father's name with your grandmother's and subtract circumcision.*
17. Nod your head but remain silent when she tells you not to compliment your child too much.
18. Continue to compliment your child but more quietly.
19. Remember that your mother waited in America at the tail end of a war between her new home and the country of her childhood, wondering what would become of her own mother, who had walked through jungles and crossed oceans to survive.
20. Watch her eyes fill with tears when she knows you or one of your siblings is in pain. Watch her lips press together, open, press together again.
21. Let her fill your plate, fill it again, and yet one more time, even if you are full.

22. Believe her when she tells you food is love.
    a. Remember that it takes hours and hours to make chả giò, and that she makes it, your favorite, without the help of her own sisters who live thousands of miles away on another continent.
    b. Agree that this is the kind of food that calls for the hands of many to prepare it.
23. Listen, listen, listen as she laments over the various ways in which she's suffered.
24. Keep listening.

SAL AND DEAN ARE DICKS

Russ?? Is this you? I have pictures of yr new daughter if u want to see her. She looks just lzqike u res[pond if you want to see her

I receive this text right before I have to teach a class. I'm not Russ, and I have no idea who he is. During class, while my students talk about the cultural tropes of masculinity in the road novel, I think about the message. Russ has a new baby! He's a father! A woman just pushed a baby into the world, and she's on a quest to find Russ! I recall the agony of giving birth to my son, and a ghost pain shoots through my pelvis.

"Sal and Dean are dicks," says one student.

"They use women like tissue!" This from a young man who has not until this moment ever spoken in class. "And don't even get me started on Sal pretending he's a migrant worker." It's clear that most of these students hate Sal, Dean, and Kerouac.

"These men are trying to escape the constraints of mainstream culture," someone pipes up from the back of the room. "Ain't nothing wrong with freedom." Apparently, there are some holdouts. I tell my students to find evidence to support their claims, lie to them about a forgotten assignment sheet in my office, and bust my phone out as soon as I'm in the hallway.

> She is tinbqy. Her fingers r so small
>
> Are u there? Russ??

An image sits below this, a red-faced infant swaddled inside one of those hospital-issue baby blankets, the tiny white ones with blue and pink stripes. The dots that pulse while someone texts appear and disappear, appear and disappear.

She is beautiful, I text back.

She is perfect, I respond.

DESTRUCTION MYTH

The first day of the rains, several cars were swept off the road in a torrent of water, sunk into the muddy ditch bottoms cradling the highway. People tried to peek through the windows of their homes at the chaos, but it was like being in a car wash—sheets of water slapping the glass, what seemed like pounding from all sides. On the coasts the oceans roared up and feasted on beachfront mansions—all glass and blinding white on one coast, shingles weathered to perfection on the other. Mudslides commenced. In the flat lands, while their basements filled with water, people flipped on the news and watched houses slip down mountains, some slow like they were moving through lava, others as fast and furious as a raft riding a chute. In the low country with its gulfs and levees, the water rose higher and higher, and people moved accordingly—first floor, to second floor, to attic, then roof, yelling at their neighbors, waving arms uselessly at the sky, soaked to the bone, the water still rising. In the cities, the people who usually scurried like mice watched the water pour down subway stairs, stood trapped in the still, stinking air of the passenger cars.

It rained so hard that animals scurried back into the wombs of their mothers. Trees bent beneath the onslaught of wind and water, spread their branches over their roots, willing themselves to stay connected to the earth. The water rose higher, and crocodiles, who swam alongside rowboats full of people, broke the surface of the water with their prehistoric heads, their heavy-lidded eyes rolling like green glass marbles. Dogs howled from rooftops, trying to signal for help along with their owners who howled louder. Women left flooding hospitals, their stomachs still swollen with babies who refused to come out, who'd gone still when the storms commenced. A tree in a city park vibrated with the screeching of hundreds of cats who clung to its limbs. The pointed faces of rats strained above the water's surface as the metro flooded. Zoo animals rode the water high enough to breach their enclosures, and on day three of the rain, a Siberian tiger swam like an Olympian through the arched entrance of a zoo somewhere in the Midwest. Deer floated along in large groups, their soft brown eyes frozen wide with fear. Three men stranded in a hunting blind cried out for their mothers.

On day four of the storms, the Pacific unhinged its mighty jaws, unrolled its tongue, and swallowed California, Oregon, and Washington in one long, satisfied gulp. Silicon Valley billionaires never escaped to their luxury bunkers in the Southern Hemisphere because their helicopters and planes, if they even got off the ground, crumpled like cheap toys in the torrential downpour. Atlantis was reborn on day five of the rain, but rather than a city, it was its own new country composed of oceanfront properties from Maine to Florida, torn from the motherland and sunk to bottom of the sea. Some day in the future, manatees, dolphin, spotted eagle rays, and bluefin tuna will flit and dive through the remains of mansions that have disintegrated in the ocean's dark depths. Clawed lobsters will watch a pod of whales use their gigantic snouts to rearrange decayed sofas, dining room tables, and the occasional grand piano. Tiny seahorses will float in teacups made of the finest bone china.

On day six of the rain, the president and all his cabinet members died in their White House bunker, stupidly going down instead of up during the flood. They drowned in the dwindling air of their tricked-out cave and cursed each other with their dying breaths. People across the land trembled and cried, made promises as they clenched their hands in prayer. Children clung to their parents' legs, climbed their mother's and father's torsos to their shoulders as the water rose higher yet. Only seven days passed before the water took the land completely, and as people—delirious with cold, hunger, and thirst—slipped beneath the surface, they remembered a burning summer day long ago and the cool relief of water as it swallowed their bodies.

NEIGHBORHOOD WATCH

In the small, neat neighborhood where the woman lives, the people next door close their shades when she pulls in her driveway, and once, when her husband comes home early from work, the neighbor lady hisses at him from her porch, "You work for the state, I'll report you!" He grins at the neighbor and flips her the bird. When he comes inside, his blue eyes are narrowed and his smile false.

The woman knows it isn't her lanky husband with his flashing blue eyes and curly blond hair who makes the neighbors cross to the other side of the street when they see the couple coming. Behind closed doors, the woman mocks the neighbors. "Provincial," she calls them. "Uneducated, ignorant pigs." She and her husband cackle. The woman and her husband met while studying in Madrid, but it's the 1970s in suburban America, and the only thing she can possibly be to her neighbors is a war bride. An intruder. A gook or chink. "Assholes," her husband says when the neighbors put up a high fence. Inside their house, the woman curses.

"Fils de pute"—*Son of a bitch*—she yells in French.

"Đi mà tự lo lấy đi!"—*Go screw yourself*—she shouts in Vietnamese.

"Pendejos"—she screams in Spanish.

"*Neak chkuot*"—Idiots—she spits in Khmer.

"Fuckers" the woman roars in English.

Fucker is her favorite English word. The woman loves the scrape of her front teeth against her bottom lip, the bursting release of that "fuh" followed by the bite of the second syllable. "Fuckers," she chants as she looks out her front window. "Fuckers," she shouts at the crisp, green lawns, the painted porch swings, the rippling American flags that surround her.

ACKNOWLEDGMENTS

Many thanks to my editor, Marisa Seigel, and the entire team at Curbstone Books and Northwestern University Press for making this collection a reality. Thanks also to my agent, Andrea Blatt, at William Morris Endeavor, who believed in this project wholeheartedly from the start. This project would not have been possible without the support of the Center for the Humanities and the College of Arts and Sciences at Drake University and of the Vermont Studio Center, whose generous grants made it possible for me to devote time and energy to these stories.

I am especially grateful to my late mother, Sophia Din Madden, who passed down her love of literature and language to me; to my father, John Madden, who shared his love of stories of all kinds with me and who continues to encourage and support my writing; and to my first and best friends, Sonia, Chris, and Margaret, for always putting up with my weirdness in childhood and presently.

Thanks to my writing crew—Michelle Ross, Kim Magowan, Beth Brinsfield, and Chrissy Kolaya—for the hellish all-day writing marathons that sparked many of these pieces. I'm grateful for my witches and fellow writers, Catherine Knepper and Jen Wilson, for helping me get through not only this book, but life in general. Thanks to Trinette and Lizzie—Rio Trio forever, and Kerri, Lindsey, and Sarah, for their life-long friendship and support. Love and gratitude to my maternal aunties and cousins who have deepened my understanding of my mother's cultural roots—and my own.

Finally, so much love and gratitude to Craig and Graham. Craig, your infinite patience and kindness are unmatched, and I could not have done this without you. And to my beautiful boy, Graham, thank you for inspiring me every single day.

Many of the stories in this collection first appeared in the journals and anthologies listed below. Thank you to all the editors of these publications for their support of my work.

Angels Flight: literary west

The Atticus Review

Bull: Men's Fiction

Cleaver, Philadelphia's international literary magazine

Cutleaf

decomP:Magazine,

Electric Literature (The Commuter)

Fiction Southeast

Flash Fiction Magazine

The Forge Literary Magazine

Fractured Literary, Action, Spectacle

Hobart

JMWW

The Masters Review: New Voices

National Flash Fiction Day Anthology

Necessary Fiction

New Flash Fiction Review,

Orchid: A Literary Review

Oxford Flash Fiction

PANK

Revolver

Word Riot

X-R-A-Y literary magazine

"Snow" first appeared in *Fairy Tale Review,* The Gold Issue, ed. Kate Bernheimer (Wayne State University Press, 2021).